NO ONE ELSE TO KILL

Special Limited Edition

FIRST EDITION

Pat,
Thanks!
Enjoy!
- Bo D

NO ONE ELSE TO KILL

Bob Doerr

TotalRecall Publications, Inc.
www.totalrecallpress.com

TotalRecall Publications, Inc.
1103 Middlecreek
Friendswood, Texas 77546
281-992-3131   281-482-5390 Fax
www.totalrecallpress.com

Printed in the United States of America with simultaneous printings in Australia, Canada, and United Kingdom.

FIRST EDITION
1   2   3   4   5   6   7   8   9   10

Thanks to all my family and friends who have supported me in my writing.

I would like to especially thank Courtney White, Keith Thomas, and Ramon Morado who contributed a little extra in this book.

Author

Bob Doerr grew up in a military family, graduated from the Air Force Academy, and had a twenty eight year career of his own in the Air Force that exposed him to the people and cultures in Asia, Europe and of these United States. Bob specialized in criminal investigations and counterintelligence gaining significant insight to the worlds of crime, espionage and terrorism. His work brought him into close contact and coordination with the FBI and CIA, along with the investigative and security agencies of many different countries. His education credits include a Masters in International Relations from Creighton University.

Now a full time author, Bob has four mystery/thrillers already published and a fifth to be released in the fall. Two of his books, Cold Winter's Kill and Loose Ends Kill, were selected as finalists for the Eric Hoffer Award. Loose Ends Kill was also awarded the 2011 Silver medal for Fiction/mystery by the Military Writers Society of America. Another Colorado Kill and Dead Men Can Kill are winners in the first quarter 2012 beta Ultimate Hero Contest.

Bob lives in Garden Ridge, Texas, with Leigh, his wife of 39 years.

Introduction

In this book Jim West finds himself traveling to a small, remote hunting lodge in the Pecos Wilderness area in New Mexico to rendezvous with an old friend and do some hiking. His friend stands him up, and Jim is about to return home when a murder occurs in the lodge. Law enforcement jumps in, and Jim's early departure plans are scrubbed. When a second murder occurs less than twenty four hours later, things really start to get dicey. Both crimes were intricately planned to mislead the authorities. Additionally, no one appears to have a motive for the killings, and everyone has an alibi. Up against a wall with time running out, the deputy-in-charge approaches West and asks him to be their man on the inside, but West is adamant that this is not his case to solve. Since his retirement from the Air Force, however, Fate has had her own plans for West. Why should this be any different?

CHAPTER 1

October 28, 1997

"**D**amn," Sean muttered to himself after stepping on a large rock and nearly twisting his ankle. He'd expected to be back to the cabin by now. In the past two years, he had made this same walk a half dozen times. This was the second journey to the small convenience store since arriving earlier in the week. He knew exactly how long the hike would take him and had started his trek with plenty of time to make it back long before dark.

Now confronted with the darkness, he admitted to himself that this trip hadn't even been necessary. However, he found the two mile hike through the forest to the store exhilarating, and the purchase of a bag of chips and some salsa would provide him with a great snack for a few days.

The trail paralleled the dirt road for a good part of the hike. This last half mile, however, took him through the thick forest. He could have followed the road while it meandered by three other cabins and a community campsite, but that would have added at least a half mile more to his hike. When he left the roadside path to take his narrow trail, the light from a nearly full moon didn't make the decision seem so foolhardy.

Unfortunately, after leaving the wide expanse of the roadway, clouds that had been non-existent all day had blown in from somewhere and now blocked most of the moon's light.

Sean felt confident that he could keep to the trail, but the darkness intimidated him. He had heard that an environmental group had released wolves in the area as part of a re-population effort. An initiative that sounded fine when he read about it from the safety of his home back in Pittsburgh, but it now made every rustle of leaves sound ominous.

The young, bleached blond clerk at the quiet little store had caused his delay.

"I'm bored," she exclaimed in response to his rhetorical "how's it going" comment when he walked by her after entering the store.

He hadn't intended on having a conversation. Yet the way she had said it, and the way her eyes had fixed on him, stopped him in his tracks as effectively as a barbed wire fence.

"You're only the second person who's been in here today," she said once she had his attention, "and my boss, who's usually here with me, had to stay home today to tend to a sick kid."

"That's too bad," Sean responded, not really knowing what to say.

"How come I haven't seen you before?" she asked, her question punctuated with a smile that drew Sean closer, like a moth to a flame.

Forty minutes had passed before Sean made it out of the store. He realized right away that he would never make it back before dark, but at the time, the flirtation had left him feeling exhilarated. Nothing would come of it. He knew he would not violate his commitment to his wife, Sandy, but still it had spiced up his day.

Now, however, he quickened his pace and wondered why he had dallied so long.

"Ooooh," a soft moan came from somewhere off to his right.

He stopped and stared into the blackness.

"Anybody out there?" he shouted. Silence.

He resumed his fast walk toward the cabin. Climbing a small rise about thirty yards further, he could see the dim light from the solar powered lamp that marked the entrance to the cabin's short driveway.

Not far now, he thought, and fought the urge to run.

A cough, no, it sounded more like muffled gagging, broke through the semi-silence of the night.

"What in God's name is out there?" Sean murmured to himself. Tomorrow he might come back and look around, but at the moment, the safety of the cabin remained his goal.

He reached the cabin's front door and had the key in his hand.

"Ooooh." This time it sounded ghostlike and closer than he liked.

He stepped inside and locked the door behind him. Instinctively, he walked around the small cabin and ensured the back door and all the windows were locked. He peered out the front window and saw nothing.

"A Halloween prank?" he asked himself aloud.

He put the chips in the cabinet and the salsa in the refrigerator, grabbing a Michelob at the same time. Picking up the latest mystery by Robert Parker, Sean sat down in the large recliner and felt his blood pressure come down a few notches.

Suddenly, something banged against the front door with a thud. Sean jumped up. He waited a few seconds before moving. Silence, again. It hadn't been a knock at the door. Whoever was out there trying to scare him had thrown something against the door. Anger replaced fear, and Sean grabbed the poker from the fireplace before moving to the front door.

"Who's out--!" Sean started to shout when he pulled the door open. At that point, Sean's life changed forever.

Everything seemed to move eerily in slow motion. He realized that the sound he now heard, which sounded less intelligible and more frightening than those he had heard earlier, erupted from his own throat.

A body had collapsed upon the door, making the thud he had heard. As the door opened, a brutalized woman fell onto his shins and feet, and her face stared up at him with open eyes that gave no indication of life. Blood drooled from her mouth and spread from a variety of wounds staining her yellow sweatshirt and blue jeans. Dirt and blood patterned her bare feet.

It took all Sean's strength to reach down and touch the woman. He had never seen her before. Could she still be alive? He had to do something, but what? He pressed his fingers against her throat looking for a pulse. Suddenly, a bloody hand shot up and grabbed his arm.

Sean's world began to spin around. He fought the dizziness and tried to sit down next to her. Then everything turned dark as he blacked out.

CHAPTER 2

October 25, 2012

"Most impressive," the tall man standing next to the white Lexus crossover said to his travelling companion.

"I like it," his friend replied. "It definitely wasn't here when I was here last."

The tall man stood next to the open driver's door. His companion had gotten out of his side of the vehicle and walked around to the open trunk.

"Afternoon," I said to the man by the trunk. I had just returned to my Mustang from inside the lodge, where I had checked in and gotten my room key.

Rather than return the greeting, the man by the trunk looked at me quizzically.

I let it go and got my suitcase out of my trunk. After I closed the trunk, I glanced over at the Lexus while I made my way back to the lodge. Both men stood together at the rear of their car, but instead of removing anything they stared at me.

"Creepy," I mumbled to myself. Putting the two of them out of my mind, I studied the front of the lodge.

"Most impressive, indeed," I thought. The lodge looked like a huge, fancy log cabin. Lengthy flower boxes lined the ground floor window sills. A large wooden bear's head growled down at anyone entering the building through the massive front doors. The doors had to be twelve feet high and nearly that wide across.   Large brass handles and knockers adorned each door. A front porch jutted out ten feet and extended about thirty feet on both sides from the main doors. A thick, highly lacquered oak hand rail lined the porch.

For practical reasons, a normal sized door stood open about fifteen feet to the right of the huge doors allowing easy access to and from the lodge. A small placard on a pedestal informed guests that for their convenience, visitors and guests should enter through the door on their right. I used the "convenient" door and reentered the lodge.

The interior of the lodge impressed me as much as the outside. Giant wooden beams adorned the ceiling, and both the registration counter and a large bar located at the east end of the first floor had been constructed with highly polished wood. Two large chandeliers hung from the ceiling, and a big window in the back of the room provided an outstanding view of the distant mountains.   The well maintained wooden flooring capped off the sensation of class.

The west end of the ground floor consisted of the dining room. I could see the sign identifying it, but unlike the bar area, the dining room was a separate room and the door to it was closed. I stopped by the registration counter again.

"You gave me room 207. Which way should I go?" The ceiling of the center portion of the ground floor, the immediate lobby area, extended up through the second floor and effectively cut the second floor into two wings. A matching set of separated stairways provided access.

"Take the stairs to the west wing, sir," the young woman behind the counter answered.

"By the way, are those real flowers out there?"

"You mean in the planters?"

"Yes," I answered. "At night, I would think it would be too cold for them."

"We bring the planters in every evening, and we only put them outside when the weather permits. At the end of the month, we'll stop putting them out at all. It's not really that much work, and the owner likes them."

"Nice touch," I said and headed off in search of my room. The tall man and his surly companion approached the counter as I walked away. I didn't bother to say anything else to them.

For all of its grand theme and near opulent façade, the Royal Lodge was not as large as I expected, nor fortunately, as expensive. On the second floor, only six rooms existed in the west wing. I imagined the east wing matched it, later discovering that wing only had five rooms. A service elevator and a utility room took the place of the sixth room.

Since the third floor ran across the entire length of the building, there could easily be another fifteen to twenty rooms up there. A note left on the desk in my room, however, apologized for any inconvenience due to the third floor being temporarily closed for repainting and new carpeting.

Other than getting the short end of the stick with the view, since my window faced the front parking lot, the room impressed me as much as the rest of the hotel had. I unpacked my suitcase and went down to the bar to get a drink and wait for Stu. His email had said his plane landed in Albuquerque at noon, and that he expected to be at the lodge between two and three.

No one except the woman behind the counter was in the bar.

"What can I get you?"

I looked over to the taps and saw they had the basics. "A Bud Light, draft, please."

She drifted over and started filling a glass. I had to smile. Of all the people, I had encountered so far, she was the first to look out of place. She had tight, short, black shorts on with those black fishnet stockings that I'd seen more often on TV or in movies than in real life. Her tight, white, short sleeve, pull over sweater completed the "look at me" outfit.

"Just get in?" she asked and placed the beer in front of me.

"Yes, just now. I'm waiting for a friend, who should be here any moment. Hope you don't mind if I hang around here to wait for him."

"I'm glad for the company. This time of day is normally slow, and now with the construction, it's been slow day and night."

"How long has it been going on?"

"Last week they had the second floor closed and this week the third floor. It's worse this week. On top of that, rumor has it that somehow word got out to the travel agencies that the lodge was going to be closed during the construction."

"Ouch, that could hurt," I said.

She leaned in closer.

"It has. I hear there's only going to be a handful of guests the rest of the week. Anyone driving by and looking at the parking lot might think we were closed." She almost whispered her remark. I wondered if the management had put out word to the staff not to discuss their current woes.

"That's too bad."

"Are you here with the hunting group?" she asked.

"No. I'm here with the two man hiking group."

She raised her eyebrows.

"You mean we didn't make the bulletin?" I smiled at her to let her know I was joking.

"Well, I did hear that we have a small group of hunters arriving here today but nothing about a group of hikers."

"Actually, I do hope we get some hiking in, but Stu and I didn't announce ourselves as any kind of a group to the lodge."

"What's your name?"

"Jim."

"Well Jim, I'm Bev. Nice to meet you."

"Likewise."

"Stick around," she said with a smile, as her eyes watched someone approach the bar. She moved off to my right.

I looked in the mirror behind the bar and saw the same two men I had seen outside approach the far end of the bar. The men had changed into matching yellow and black, Pittsburgh Steelers sweatshirts. Bev approached them, but her smile didn't draw a similar response. She mixed two drinks for them and moseyed back to me.

"Sourpusses," she grumbled.

"I saw them outside. I don't know what's the matter with them, but they aren't too chatty, that's for sure."

Bev and I talked for the next two hours. She claimed to have a vagabond's background: married three times but not at the moment, no regular job, and never lived anywhere in her life more than a couple of years. An only child of parents who divorced shortly after her birth, she bounced between mom, dad, grandparents, and even an aunt. When she got old enough, she soon made a mess of her adult life. I didn't argue her point. After trying not to hear about her three years with a motorcycle gang and two years in Mexico as a missionary, I successfully changed the topic to the hotel business.

She asked me about my life, a topic which I adroitly avoided. I did mention my dog, Chubbs, left at home under the close watch of my neighbors' children. That sufficed for information about me. She enjoyed gossiping about other personalities on the staff and about rumors she had heard concerning the lodge's pending financial ruin. Nice enough woman, and not bad to look at, but if I had had anything else to do at all I would have left long ago.

I swallowed the last ounce of beer from my third glass and looked around the hotel lobby. No sign of Stu, and for that matter I didn't see anyone other than the hotel staff.

"Bev, if you'll excuse me, I need to go see what happened to my friend, Stu."

"Sure, Jim. Don't be a stranger."

I walked over to the reception desk and asked them if they had a message for me. They didn't. In fact, they hadn't received any message from a Mr. Winston. I stepped out onto the front porch.

The unseasonably warm afternoon fought its losing battle with the cool evening air. A man in overalls carried rows of flowers around to the back of the building. A small charter bus pulled into the parking lot. I watched for Stu to get off, but didn't see him in the gaggle of men and women who did. They walked into the lodge laughing and talking loudly while the driver struggled with the plethora of luggage and rifle cases.

The hunters, I thought, and dialed Stu's number on my cell phone. He answered on the third ring.

"Stu, where are you?"

"At home," he paused. "Sorry, Jim, I went to the airport but changed my mind at the last minute. Just couldn't motivate myself to get on the airplane. Maybe some other time."

"Hey man, this trip was for you. Not me. You need to get out. I know how you feel--"

"No you don't. Your wife and kid didn't die."

Low blow, I thought. He had no right to try to make me feel guilty. I forced myself to count to ten, well, maybe to three.

"You're right Stu. You take your time. I'll talk to you later." I hung up. "Damn," I said to myself.

I looked around and leaned against the handrail. I could hear the trees move with the breeze, but everything else was silent. I hadn't planned this trip and had always felt that I shouldn't have let myself be talked into it. In fact, I probably should've expected something like this.

Stu's sister, Angie, had done all the arranging and arm twisting. My ex and I had become friends with Stu and his wife, Serena, during our Air Force assignment in D.C. They lived across the street from us. Angie lived a few miles away in Fairfax, Virginia. At the time, both Stu and I worked at the Pentagon. For the two years I lived there, we carpooled to work and became close friends. Stu, a civil engineer, had the thankless job of being the number two guy in charge of making sure that the Pentagon worked. Not the people in it; that might have been an impossible job at times. Rather, his office ensured the lights worked, the roof didn't leak, and the toilets flushed. I couldn't have handled it.

Angie spent a lot of time at Stu's place, and as a result, we had become friends. I hadn't stayed in touch with either Stu or his sister since my own divorce and was therefore surprised when the email from her arrived on my computer about two months ago.

The email informed me of the accident that resulted in the death of Stu's wife and child. A large truck had run into their small car. Stu was at work when he got the call. Angie explained that Stu hadn't been the same since. I remember thinking, "Who would be?" She said that he rarely went to work anymore and had lost at least twenty pounds in the months since the accident. She gave me his phone number and asked me to call him. She thought that talking to me might help.

I wanted to ask how talking to me could help, and I didn't want to call him. I felt sorry for him, but I didn't think my calling him would help. My email back to her expressed my sympathy, and despite my feelings I said I would call.

Since then, I'd had three phone conversations with Stu, two initiated by him. I had also talked to Angie twice. She called both times. I hadn't felt like my conversations with Stu had been worthwhile, but she thought they had been. She said he really needed to get away for a few days, and that meant not only away from the D.C area, but from her and his immediate circle of friends.

I remember wanting to ask, "What's that got to do with me?" I didn't, and to my chagrin she told me anyway.

"Jim, Stu's always wanted to go hiking in the Rockies. As you know, he's done a lot of it in the Appalachians, but has never been out west. If I can talk him into making a trip out there, just for a couple of days, would you meet him and go hiking with him?"

"He doesn't seem to be interested in doing anything, Angie. What makes you think he would go hiking with me?"

"He used to always talk about it, and I found this neat lodge on the internet near Lake Katherine in the Pecos Wilderness Area. You know, there in New Mexico. Just say you'll do it, and I'll work on him. He likes you, and maybe he'll agree to do it. Please?"

"Will you come, too?" I asked. It slipped out before I could stop it.

"You do this for him, and me, and maybe next time I'll come out."

She had me hooked. I always had this unspoken thing for her. I don't think she knew it, nor would I have wanted her to. I was married back then, and she had gone through husbands like Baskin Robbins goes through flavors.

"Okay, I'll give it a shot."

"It'll have to be fairly short notice. If he has time to dwell on the idea, he'll back out. I understand you're not working now?" I'm pretty sure that's what she said, but I heard "You don't have a life now anyway."

"Yeah, I guess I'm available anytime." Ouch. I might as

well put a big "L" on my forehead.

Her tone changed after hearing my response, "How are you doing, Jim?"

"Fine. Hey, I have another call," I lied. "Let me know what he says." I hung up. I didn't need her sympathy turned toward me.

CHAPTER 3

The dining room opened at five. However, at quarter past, when I entered, I had my choice of any table and chair in the place. No one stood guard at the entrance to seat me or to check to see if I had a reservation. No one brought any water out to me. I wondered if I had misread the opening time.

The place looked nice enough, just completely devoid of life. After waiting two or three minutes, I walked back out to the reception desk to ensure they hadn't closed the dining room during the ongoing construction. After being reassured it was open, I went back to my table.

This time one of the serving staff showed up right away. The reception clerk had probably warned them. I ordered the small steak and started a debate with myself whether to head back home tomorrow or to spend a day hiking as planned. With Stu now an absentee, I wished I had brought along Chubbs, my faithful mutt. He would enjoy a day walking through the forest.

About the same time my meal arrived, a lone, older gentleman walked in, looked around at the twenty or so tables, and picked the one right next to me.

"Too shy to join me?" I wanted to ask but didn't in case he thought I meant it.

"Beautiful day out there, don't you think?" he asked me.

"Sure is," I said and looked back at my steak.

He didn't take the hint. "Did you see the flowers outside on the windows?"

"Yes, quite colorful."

"They must not be real. They could never survive the cold."

"That's what I thought, but the hotel staff takes them inside when it gets dark and only puts them out when the weather permits."

"Nice touch. Have you been here for a while?"

"Just got in today."

"Are you here for the hunting?" he asked.

"No, the hiking."

"Great hunting here. At least there was last year."

I didn't take the bait, but I did take a bite of my steak.

"Yeah, last year we came to check the place out. Had a great time. Where you from?"

"Clovis."

"Been there. Not much to do there. What do you do?"

I had two choices. While I would have liked to have eaten my meal in silence and then return to my room, I decided not to fight the inevitable.

"I'm retired Air Force, name's Jim West."

"I'm Cross Benson; nice to meet you Jim. Since we're both alone, do you mind if I join you?" He stood up and started moving before I could say anything. I motioned for him to sit across from me. He sat in the chair next to me.

"Where are you in from, Cross?"

"El Paso.   We all are. I run a commercial real estate enterprise. The rest of the gang makes up most of my key staff. A couple times a year, I like to get us away from the office."

"Probably a good idea. I think I saw your group when you arrived."

"You did. You were out front. I remember you. You aren't here by yourself, are you?"

"Good question. I wasn't supposed to be," I said.

"Woman problems?"

I smiled. "Not this time. The guy I was supposed to meet here couldn't make it. Unfortunately, I didn't find out until after I arrived."

"Hey, you're welcome to join us."

"Thanks, Cross, but I haven't even made up my mind yet if I'm staying tomorrow."

The server came, brought Cross a glass of wine, and took his order. He ordered the big steak.

I took advantage of the break in conversation to eat some more of my dinner. I started to reach for my glass of water when I realized Cross was taking a big gulp out of it. I looked over at his table and saw his glass of water. He must have thought he brought the glass with him, but since I didn't have anything else in front of me to drink, it shouldn't have been difficult for him to figure out the water wasn't his.

"If I remember right, this place has great food," he said.

"This steak is good," I admitted. I wanted to add that my water wasn't bad either.

The server returned to our table..

"Hold on," he instructed. "Jim, do you drink wine?"

"Sure."

"Well, you need to try this. Discovered it myself at the Heritage Oak Winery out in the Sacramento area. It's a Zinfandel, but all their wines are excellent. Can I offer you a glass?"

"Sure," I said to him, and after he instructed the server to bring us another glass of wine, I asked for another glass of water. Cross had no reaction to my request for another water, but the waiter looked at me quizzically and then at Cross' original table. He smiled to himself and walked away.

"Last year, I saw that they carried this line of wine. I told them to keep it on their wine list. I'm glad to see that they did."

"How long are you all planning to stay here?"

"Four nights. We'll head back south on Monday. This trip is always stag, no spouses. The spring is with spouses, so we make a full week out of it. Did a cruise out of Galveston this year. Fun, but seems like when the spouses are along there's a lot more stress. We have one husband and five wives that make the spring trip. You'd be surprised; we get as much whining from the one husband as we do from all the wives."

"I believe it."

"One rule on the fall trip, though. What goes on in this trip, stays on this trip. I don't mean to imply we're a very wild group, because, believe me, we're not."

From the looks of Cross, closer to seventy than sixty, and not in very good shape, I wondered how wild they could get.

"A good rule to have," I said, not meaning it at all.

"It's a good group. I'll have to introduce you to Randi.

She's the one without a husband. Although just between you and me, you might have just as much luck with Geri."

I assumed Geri was another woman, but ignored his comment anyway.

His dinner came out and our conversation dwindled while I finished my meal and Cross attacked his. I had to admit the wine tasted excellent. I ordered a second glass without any prompting.

All in all, Cross wasn't bad company. We drank coffee and discussed the current woes in the commercial real estate business after our plates had been taken away.

"If you're shrewd," he said, "there's still money to be made out there. Just not as much as there was a few years ago," he paused, and I thought he had finished with his comment. Then he said softly, almost to himself, "but you still have to watch your back."

The rest of his group entered the dining room. They were loud and unsteady. More than likely, they had come directly from the bar.

"I had to give up everything but a little red wine. It's probably a blessing," he remarked in response to seeing his companions.

For him or them, I wondered.

"Doctor's orders, you know," he said.

I nodded, but of course I didn't.

"And, my wife's quite the enforcer. Goes overboard if I simply look too long at a glass of scotch, but I have to admit that I feel a lot better now that I'm off all that stuff. Are you married, Jim?"

"Not anymore," I didn't elaborate.

His turn to nod. Give him credit for not asking me about it.

"Hey Cross, who's your new friend here?"

I had watched her break away from the rest of the group while they were being seated and come our way. She had a medium build, medium height, and medium looks. Her mid-length cut brown hair was closer to a true brown than seemed normal for hair. Not too dark or too light. She wore brown slacks and a tan pullover sweater. Yet in the middle of this blandness, she had painted her lips a glaring red; almost a scary red against her pale skin.

"Randi, how's it going?"

"Great."

"This is Jim West. I only met him this evening, but I already like him."

He reached over and gave my shoulder a friendly slap. She simply smiled at me.

"Yeah, we even shared water," I said to her lips. Somehow, I knew my comments confused them, and I even wondered why I said it. I forced myself to take my eyes off her mouth. "I meant some wine. Cross gave me a great recommendation for the wine."

He beamed.

"How's the food this year?" she asked.

"Great," he said.

"It really is," I seconded.

"Well, I better get back. I just wanted to say hi. You both enjoy your dinners."

"Nice meeting you, Randi," I said. She smiled and left.

"A hard worker, that one is."

"What does she do?"

"Marketing. Smartest thing I ever did was to hire her away from her brother."

We talked a little more after we finished eating. He had a wealth of knowledge on the local area despite being from El Paso.

"What do you think was the largest town in North America some four hundred years ago?" he asked.

Figuring it had to be a local city, I said, "Santa Fe."

"No but good guess. It was the town of Pecos."

"Pecos? You mean the small town up the road?"

"Not quite. The original Pecos is just a bunch of ruins now, but also nearby. Coronado, the early Spanish explorer used the small Indian town as a stopping point and the Spanish stayed. It became quite the mission and regional hub. It kind of died away over time and by the mid 1800's was totally abandoned."

"Disease?"

"No more than elsewhere. It was pretty much destroyed during an Indian uprising in the late 1600's. Disease, drought and more Indian raids had their toll after that. Another big factor was that the Spanish government had moved their governing apparatus to Santa Fe and then lost control of the area all together. The city withered away. The ruins are still an interest to archaeologists and historians."

"What Indian tribes were here then?"

"Different ones. The Spanish referred to them as Pueblo Indians because they lived in small towns, or pueblos. I think the Hopi and Zuni tribes were the largest up here, but you know over the years the Indians seized each others' lands. Hell, the white man didn't do anything different than the Indians had done to each other over the centuries. It's just that we were able to hang on to it. By we, I don't mean the Spanish either. The strong have always taken from the weak. It's nature's way."

"I know," I said.

"What I find interesting, though, is that we accepted most of the Spanish names for the area out here rather than create new ones, like the Spanish did, or why we didn't go back to the original Indian names. For example, we still call the mountains out here the Sangre de Cristo Mountains."

I knew the Sangre de Cristo Mountains were part of the Rocky Mountain chain but not much more.

"And, did you know the only significant Civil War battle in New Mexico happened near here?"

"Yeah, now that you mentioned it, I do recall it took place around or near the Glorietta Pass. I'm impressed with your knowledge of the local area, Cross."

"It's a hobby."

Cross did most the talking, but after a while, I noticed that he had already glanced a couple of times at his group, and I figured he was ready to join them. I made an excuse to leave and thanked him for the conversation. I hadn't expected to, but I had actually enjoyed his company.

While I made my way out of the dining room, I looked over at Cross' group. Randi smiled and gave me a little wave. Her camouflage blended in so well with a large cabinet behind her that when I saw her smile it reminded me of those Disney animations where the Cheshire cat smiled and all you saw was the smile.

She might have made an interesting painting, but if her aim was to be provocative, she shot past that to the spooky category.

I stared at her a little too long and almost ran into Frick and Frack, the two men wearing the Steelers sweatshirts.

"Excuse me," I said and eased around them at the doorway. They both stared at me like I was the one wearing the fire engine red lipstick. Neither said a thing. If I hadn't heard them talking to each earlier in the parking lot, I might have thought they were mute.

I contemplated having one last drink at the bar before retiring to my room. Bev gave me a flirtatious wave which excited the usual conflicting emotions. A buzz from my phone saved me from having to make a decision. I waved back at Bev and walked out to the front porch. A gust of cold wind ripped through my clothing and took away any warmth I had dared to bring outside with me.

"Jim," the female voice in my phone said to me.

"Hey Angie," I said.

"He's still here. He didn't go."

"I know. I guess he got cold feet."

"That's no excuse. He needs to move on with his life."

I didn't say anything. What was I supposed to say? I waited her out.

"I'm worried about him," she said and paused again.

I gave in. "You need to let it go, Angie, or you'll get as obsessed about him as he is about his loss. He doesn't appear to be willing to let anyone else help him, so he's going to have to work through this himself."

"I'm sorry I dragged you into this."

"That's all right," I lied.

"Are you at the lodge?"

"Yes."

"Let me pay the hotel bill. It's the least I can do."

"No. I can cover it easy enough. I'm just staying the night anyway."

"I'm sorry, Jim."

"Me, too."   We said our goodbyes.

I returned to my room.

CHAPTER 4

My toilet flushed. Not usually a very noteworthy event, I admit. However, the only light in the room came from the radio/clock on the night stand next to my head. It read three o'clock, and I was supposed to be alone. I could barely see through the darkness to the bathroom door or to the door that led out to the hallway. They both appeared shut.

I scanned the rest of the room. It appeared empty. I climbed out of bed still holding my pillow. Not much of a weapon, but it was all I had. The sound of the water filling the toilet tank finished and silence once again reigned. I crept to the bathroom door and listened. Nothing.

In the movies, they always show the door being opened slowly. Not my style, and unless you're absolutely sure you can do so without making a sound, which is almost impossible, it's a risky way to approach a possible threat in such a small place. I took hold of the door as quietly as possible, and then in one swift movement, opened it, and bolted inside determined to surprise, if not scare, the person inside.

Empty. I switched on the light and walked around my entire room. I even looked in the closet.

"Now that's weird," I said out loud.

I turned off the lights and climbed back into the bed. Could it have been the toilet in an adjoining room? I didn't think so. The silence in the room almost had me back asleep when I again heard something.

I sat up. The sound, barely audible, crept in from somewhere outside the room. I recognized the sound I heard right away. Somewhere in the hotel, someone was crying. Not a loud wailing cry but rather a low soft sob. It sounded like it came from a man, although I couldn't be sure. I rolled over and tried to ignore it, but it didn't go away. It suddenly dawned on me that the crying sounded like it came from above me, and that didn't make sense. The third floor was closed off for construction.

Already agitated over my self-flushing toilet mystery, I decided I could at least solve, as Dr. Watson might have titled it, "The Mystery of the Sobbing Man." I put on my jeans and wandered out into the hallway. The lighting had been dimmed in the hallway but was sufficient to allow me to easily see that no one was out and about on the entire second floor. The crying seemed to have stopped, but I had come this far and decided to take a peek at the third floor.

A door at the end of my hallway, only a few paces away from my room, gave me access to the stairs that led to the third floor. A similar door on the third floor had a sheet of paper taped to it warning people to stay out due to the ongoing construction. I ignored it and pushed the door open.

As the door swung open, I heard, just for a second, the sound of a man crying again. The door made a loud creaking sound when it was about two thirds open. I held the door still and waited. The crying stopped. The hallway lights were out and tarps that hung off a number of ladders scattered throughout the hall blocked most of my view of the first twenty or thirty feet of the hall that the light from the stairwell illuminated. The more distant ladders could almost be people draped in sheets. Spooky, I thought.

I looked around for a light switch but didn't see one. Soft footsteps broke the otherwise total silence.

"Hello. Is everything alright?" No one answered. I heard what sounded like a door opening and shutting at the other end of the long hallway. A glimmer of light briefly entered the hall from the far end. My view was partially blocked, and I had the sense that the door had only been opened wide enough to allow a person to sneak through.

I stood still for a few seconds. Silence and darkness dominated my senses until a faint odor of cigarette smoke drifted by me. If I'd had a flashlight and a lot more nerve, I might have explored the floor. Someone could still be up here, but I doubted it. Whoever it was had left upon my arrival, so I retreated to my room.

To calm my jittery nerves, I rechecked my entire room for anything out of the ordinary before climbing back into bed. Just before I fell back asleep the howling of a distant wolf or coyote gently broke the silence.

It's a rare morning when my eyes don't open within a few minutes of seven, and in fairness, my middle of the night escapade around the hotel may have thrown me out of cycle. However, when I opened my eyes and saw that the bedside clock said eight thirty, I initially thought the clock was broken.

My cell phone surprised me by agreeing with the clock.

I skipped shaving.   After all this was supposed to be a vacation and more importantly, I didn't want to miss breakfast.

Once again, I had the dining room to myself. I saw evidence that other tables had been used that morning, but no one else had selected the late shift for breakfast. A different waiter than I had seen the night before came up to my table. He looked at his watch before he addressed me.

I had the feeling he wanted to tell me I had missed breakfast.

"Coffee?"

"Yes, please."

"Would you like to see a menu?"

"Sure," I said, and he drifted away in disappointment.

A figure caught my eye at the door. I didn't recognize her at first. Decked out in all black, black hair, and if my eyes didn't deceive me at this distance, black lipstick. She wore a metal chain of some sort around her neck. Tight black jeans reached down to her black, spiked heels.

She waved at me and approached my table. Fascinating. The lady had guts. Whether she had taste, I couldn't be sure. After all, this was all out of my league, and I had missed out on the Goth era. I managed a smile.

"Morning, Randi. Would you like to join me?

"Hey, Jimmy. How are you this morning?"

"Fine," I stood up and pulled out a chair. "Have a seat."

"No thanks. Sounds nice, but I just came by for a big mug of coffee."   Her eyes stared at me. I don't think they blinked. Luckily, the waiter returned to my rescue.

"Here, take mine. I can get another."

"Well, thanks, Jimmy. Maybe we could do lunch," she said and walked away.

We both watched her leave.

"That is one hot babe," the young man next to me said.

"I hear she's single," I said.

"Might be, but when she was in here earlier, half the men in her group were hitting on her."

"How about getting me another cup of coffee, and do you have cinnamon rolls?"

"Yes."

"Then I'll just have a cinnamon roll with the coffee."

"Want the cinnamon roll heated?"

"Please."

While I waited for my breakfast, I thought about Randi. Cross hadn't implied she might be a little weird. Last night's look struck me as weird, but it hadn't fazed Cross. This morning's look ranged more in the bizarre category. I could see it in a misguided teenager, but I placed Randi somewhere around forty.

"Here you go, sir." He put the coffee and roll in front of me on the table.

"Was she wearing that same outfit this morning at breakfast?"

"Yeah. Hot, wasn't it?"

"Yeah," I said just to be agreeable. "I heard the same group came here last year. Did you work here then?"

"No, I've only been here two months."

A gun shot and then another echoed in from somewhere outside.

"That sounded close," I said.

"The lodge has a private range where customers can sight and check their rifles. Don't worry. There are a bazillion safety rules they have to follow."

A few more shots that sounded like they came from high powered rifles were followed by one that sounded like a small caliber one.

"It could get noisy around here," I said.

"The range is only open from nine to nine thirty in the morning."

"Not much time."

He shrugged and walked back to the kitchen. I heard a couple more shots from high powered rifles, but that was all. I imagined having its own limited use firing range was a plus for a lodge trying to attract hunters.

I finished my cinnamon roll, which was a bit of a letdown, got a second cup of coffee, and went out on the front porch. The sunshine almost overwhelmed me at first, and I had to cup my free hand over my eyes as they tried to adjust. It felt too warm to be the end of October. I decided to stay one more day and take a long hike through the forest.

A dark van with tinted windows pulled into the parking lot from a dirt road that joined the lot on the near side. It parked nearly in front of me and Cross' group climbed out of it. They were carrying rifle cases and ribbing one another for their lack of success in hitting the targets they had apparently used to sight their rifles. Randi and Cross were absent from the group.

"Morning," one of the men said to me as they passed.

"Great day isn't it?" said another to me.

"Sure is," I acknowledged. I wondered if Randi and Cross didn't feel a need to check out their rifles or if they even hunted. I thought Cross did from the comments he had made at dinner, but I had no idea about Randi. I smiled to myself as I imagined the different outfits she might wear if she did.

Suddenly, a piercing scream burst through the open doorway to the lodge, followed by another and then a third.

I hurried inside and saw a flood of people rushing down the ground floor hallway. I didn't rush, but I did follow the gaggle into the east wing. A crowd had formed at the end of the hall. Everyone seemed to be staring into the last room on the left. One of the hotel staff held a crying Randi in his arms.

The receptionist who had checked me in ran past me to the front desk. I followed her. She grabbed a phone on the counter and dialed 911.

"We need help. One of our guests has been shot. I think he may be dead," she paused. "Yes, that's us. Do you know how to get here?" Another pause, "I don't think we have any doctors here." She looked up at me, and I shook my head. "Yes," a long pause, "no, no, okay, I understand. Please hurry."

She hung up and rushed by me, heading back to the scene.

I considered getting my stuff and heading straight back to Clovis at this point. This didn't involve me. My feet had a mind of their own, however, and before I could drive any common sense down to them, I found myself standing among the crowd just outside the door to what looked like an office.

I squeezed by enough of the crowd to see two men from the hotel staff and one man from the hunting group stretching Cross out on the rug and trying to administer first aid. From my position, I couldn't see a wound on Cross or any blood in the room.

Randi started crying louder again. Geri, the other female in the hunting group, had taken over comforting duties.

"Now, now," Geri said softly. "Let's get you back to your room."

They started their weave through the small crowd, but as they passed me, Randi looked up at me and collapsed. She fell more into my arms than toward the floor. I held her upright, steadying her.

"Whoa, girl," Geri said. She looked at me. "Sorry about that, but seeing as she's attached to you, would you mind helping me get her to her room?"

A scent of perfume wafted by and through the middle of the chaos got my attention. Randi was about as close to me as you can get with your clothes on, and Geri came attached to one of Randi's arms, so she wasn't much further away. I guessed the perfume belonged to Geri. Whereas Randi dressed unusual, Geri looked sharp in her pressed khaki slacks and turquoise sweater.

"No problem, lead the way," I said.

"I'm dizzy," Randi mumbled after we had only taken a few steps.

"Here," I said and picked her up. She was surprisingly light in my arms. I followed Geri to a room on the east wing of the second floor. She opened the room with a card key.

"Her room?"

"No, actually it's my husband's and mine. Put her on the bed."

I did and noticed Randi's eyes were open and focused at me.

"Someone shot him," she said.

"I didn't see a wound."

"It was right here," she touched the back of her head. "Who would do such a thing?"

"I don't know."

"Here's a drink of water. Sit up a little." Geri moved in close to her, and I took a step away. The perfume definitely belonged to her. After Randi took a sip of water and placed her head back down on the pillow, Geri began to gently rub her face and neck with a wet wash cloth she'd brought over with the glass of water.

"That feels good," Randi said. She unbuttoned the top two buttons of her blouse and Geri expanded her massaging with the wash cloth.

"Try to get some rest, Randi. If you're up to it, maybe we'll do that lunch after all." I left the room feeling a little uncomfortable. I didn't have a big desire to eat lunch with Randi, but despite the rational part of my brain telling me to stay out of it, my curiosity of what she discovered in that room had gotten the better of me.

CHAPTER 5

By the time I got back downstairs, the first of the emergency responders had arrived, and I could hear the sirens of more close behind.

A man who I had not seen before, but I felt pretty sure was the manager of the lodge, stood at the entry to the hall and instructed hotel guests and staff to vacate the hallway.

"You do not need to return to your rooms, but this hallway needs to be cleared for the ambulance and the police. The dining room will be serving coffee and snacks for anyone who wants them, free of charge." The manager also passed instructions to his staff as they passed him, but I couldn't make out what he said.

I went into the dining room. The hunting group gathered at one big table. The two men I had observed upon my arrival were either in their rooms or out somewhere as I had not seen either of them all morning. I didn't know if the hotel had other guests or not.

Rather than be antisocial, I strolled over to the big table, too. Besides, I wanted to know what they thought had just happened. I hadn't heard any shots that sounded like they came from inside the lodge.

"Do you mind if I join you?" I asked.

None of the friendliness that they had been so full of before was present now.

"This may not be the best time," the chubby one with the burr haircut said.

"Hell, what does it matter? Let him sit down," said the one with the permanent five o'clock shadow.

None of the others seconded his opinion.

"Go ahead and sit down, Jim." Geri had come in behind me and cast the deciding vote.

"Thanks. I felt it would be awkward to sit alone a few tables away after what just happened." Actually, I was just nosy but didn't think that would sound the same.

"How's Randi?" asked the one who always needed a shave.

"She'll be alright," Geri answered. "I asked one of the EMS guys to check her out when they had a chance, but other than the shock of finding Cross, she's fine. In fact, if it wasn't for that, I would've thought she was faking, the way she swooned into Jim's arms out there."

"No time to be joking, Geri," said the burr haircut.

"Sorry, dear. By the way, have you all met Jim?"

One member of the group said no. They all looked at me.

"I'm Jim West. Sorry we couldn't have met under better circumstances."

"You must have been here when Cross was killed?" It didn't sound like a simple, innocent question. The asker looked like years ago he could've played professional ball – any of the big three. He still looked in good shape, but the grey hair and lines in his face put him close to sixty.

"Before we give him the third degree, let me introduce each of you," Geri said.

"Hey, someone just killed Cross. He wasn't just our boss, he was our friend.   I, for one, don't feel like being social," remarked burr haircut.

"I understand that, but there is no reason to be hostile to anyone at this point." I wondered what she meant by "at this point." No one contradicted her.

"My husband, Vic." She motioned with an open hand toward burr haircut.   "Next to him on his right is Mark Stallings." The guy needing a shave nodded. "Between you and Mark is Tom Griffith." He hadn't said anything yet. I noticed he had a diamond stud in his right ear. "This is Aaron Nesbitt," she touched the man's arm to her left. He was the former athlete. "Last, but not least, is Harv." She motioned toward one of the group who had Mexican features. I wondered why she hadn't offered his last name. He hadn't said anything since I joined them. Harv at least gave me a half smile with his half nod.

"Nice to meet you all, and again, I'm sorry about Cross."

"I can't believe it," Harv remarked softly. He sounded sincere, and I knew he meant Cross' death, not my expression of sympathy.

The manager entered the dining room and approached our table.

"I'm so sorry. I just can't believe this happened here." I could see the stress in his face. Small beads of sweat had popped out on his forehead. "I meant what I said. Anything you want from the kitchen, just ask for it. I'll make sure the staff knows it's on the house."

"How about from the bar?" Stallings asked the question.

"Later. The cop in charge said no to the alcohol."

Someone to my right grumbled. I didn't blame the police for not wanting us to start drinking, but I wondered about their authority in not allowing us to have one. Since I didn't want one, I didn't push the issue.

"Are you the manager of this place?" Geri asked.

"Yes, and I do appreciate your patience with us."

"One could hardly blame you or the lodge for what happened," Geri replied.

"Who is to blame?" her husband sniped. Geri gave him a look. I began to feel all wasn't content between them. Perhaps Cross' comments about my having better luck with Geri than Randi might have been more serious than I took it.

"The killer, dear. The killer."

"So it wasn't suicide?" I asked.

"What?" Vic asked.

"I mean, well," I paused, "have the police ruled out suicide?"

"Oh come on, Cross would more likely have shot one of us than himself," Griffith finally spoke up. Harv nodded in agreement.

"I saw the wound. It was in the back of his head. Not a likely spot for a suicide. Besides, while I didn't exactly look for one, I didn't see a gun in the room," stated Nesbitt, the member of the hunting troop in with the staff trying to perform CPR. With the distraction Randi caused, I couldn't be sure.

A uniformed, New Mexico state patrolman walked into the dining room. He carried a clipboard.

"May I have your attention please? I simply need to ensure we have everyone's names, addresses, phone numbers. You know: the basics. I have a list from the hotel that I can work from, but I need you to verify the information."

The patrolman appeared to be in his early twenties. He looked at us. No one said anything.

"Sure," I said. Maybe he thought he needed permission.

"Ok," he said. "Victor and Geri Schutte," he looked around.

"That's us," Geri answered.

"1214 Tapaz Court, El Paso, 555-575-3432."

"Correct."

The patrolman continued rattling off names and data of the entire hunting group, only skipping Cross and Randi. Good prep work, I thought. Not only did they get the info before he came into the room, he knew who to expect in the room.

"And you're Mr. West, right?"

"Yes."

He rattled off my contact info, and I acknowledged he had it right.

"Do any of you know where we can find a Sean or Colt Bettes?"

"Never heard of them," Geri responded.

"They're the other two guests at the lodge right now."

Frick and Frack, I thought. At least they had real names.

"I think I know who you're talking about, but I haven't seen them at all this morning," I said.

"If you all could stay here for a few more minutes, Sheriff Montoya will be with you in a bit."

The patrolman hadn't even reached the door when Geri

turned toward me. "Do you think they killed Cross?"

"I have no idea."

"It's only a matter of numbers," Vic said. "The six of us were down at the range when Cross was murdered. That only leaves the two of them and your friend here."

I didn't react to his dumb inference. "Actually, you forgot the entire lodge staff, Randi, and anyone else who may have been in the lodge at the time."

"He's right, Vic," Stallings said. Vic gave him a nasty look. No love lost between those two, I thought. That was the second time Stallings sided with me over Vic, and I didn't even know the guy.

"Jim, right?" Stallings asked.

"Yeah."

"Do you know those two guys?"

"No. They arrived yesterday when I did. I just saw them. That's all."

"I can't believe someone actually murdered Cross," Geri said. "This only happens in the movies."

"Don't you watch the news? You know we share a border with Juarez, the world's murder capital. These things, unfortunately, do happen." Harv didn't come across being short with Geri. He just sounded matter-of-fact.

"Did he have enemies over there?" I asked.

"No," Geri responded, and the rest nodded or at least didn't disagree.

"I don't know anyone who would've had a motive," Nesbitt added. "We may have some competitors who don't care for us and maybe some angry, past clients, but no one….." he left his sentence unfinished.

"Oh my God," Harv said softly. "Who's going to call Bea?"

They looked at each other. No one stepped up to the plate.

"Is Bea Cross' wife?" I asked

"Yeah, been married forever," he said.

"I vote we let the police do it. It's their job anyway, isn't it?" Vic's comments only deepened my dislike for the guy.

Nobody spoke for a minute or two. The silence broke when two members of the wait staff showed up. Despite the events of the morning, or perhaps because of them, most at the table ordered large breakfasts. Nesbitt ordered a cheeseburger. Only Geri declined.

"I can't eat anything right now," she said.

My gut told me she meant it.

"I don't mean to sound morbid, but what happens to the company now?" Griffith asked.

"It'll continue," Geri said.

"But, I mean, his death has to have an impact. Cross was the senior partner."

"I'm not absolutely certain," Geri added, "but I sat in on the legal briefing we had a few years back when Cross updated a few things. We do have a transition plan. We have insurance for this type of--"

"Insurance? Why wouldn't that go to his family?" Nesbitt interrupted.

"I have no doubt that there's insurance that the family will be getting, too. In fact, if my memory serves me right, the insurance the company has on Cross is to help us compensate his wife in exchange for her releasing her interest in it. Cross got it to help us get through this sort of thing."

"Are you a partner, Geri?" I asked.

"Yes. I own twenty per cent. There's another partner who's not here."

"That's old man Hardzog, right?" Vic asked.

"Yes, he also owns twenty per cent. He actually owned the company outright before Cross bought him out years ago. Mr. Hardzog isn't active in the company anymore, although he does sit on the board."

"Do we get any money out of this insurance?" Stallings asked. He noticed a couple of critical stares. "It's just a curiosity question, that's all."

"I'm not sure. I mean it's not that type of insurance, but it's there so none of us lose anything. If it ensures we stay in business and stay profitable, that helps, but we'll need the lawyers to explain it all to us."

"Shouldn't one of us call Sheila?" Griffith asked.

"I guess so," Geri responded.

"I don't think we should call anyone until the police tells us it's okay," Stallings said. "And then, I think we should call Bea before we call Sheila."

"Who's Sheila?" I asked.

"Cross' personal assistant. She's been with him since he became the boss," Geri answered.

CHAPTER 6

Sheriff Robert Montoya arrived at our table at the same time as our meals did. He looked disheveled and weary. I wondered if he had been up all night. After introducing himself and thanking us for our patience, he told us we needed to stay at the lodge for the remainder of the day unless we were specifically released by him.

"Sheriff," Vic said, "we were supposed to start our hunting today. You can't –"

"Vic! Cross has been killed. NO ONE is going hunting today!" Geri's vehement reproach silenced Vic. Their eyes met with obvious hostility.

"As I said, I'm sorry, but I must insist you each remain available to speak with my investigators today."

"Is Cross really dead?" Harv asked. "I mean you can officially say it, right?"

"Yes, he is –"

"He was shot, right Sheriff?" Harv asked.

"The details will come out later. I don't want to say this or that happened until I hear the official version myself."

"When should we expect to be interviewed?" Stallings asked.

"This morning. We'll get started this morning, but some of you may not get called until afternoon."

"It shouldn't take long. It's not like we have much to say," Vic grumbled.

Sheriff Montoya glanced at a notepad. "Do any of you have any idea where we can reach either Sean or Colt Bettes?"

Everyone replied either by saying no or shaking their heads.

The sheriff left and conversation dwindled as we all focused on our food. I noticed a few furtive glances that members of the group shot back and forth to each other, but their importance, if any, was lost on me.

Before I had finished eating, four deputies entered the dining room. The deputy on the far left called for Geri and left the room with her and one other deputy. While they departed, one of the remaining deputies asked for Vic. The two deputies led him out a moment later.

"We don't have to stay right here all day, do we?" Nesbitt asked. His question was not addressed to anyone in particular.

"I don't know," Griffith responded.

"I think they want us to be available to them. My guess, that's anywhere here at the lodge."

"Good, because I'm going to my room." He walked off carrying his mug of coffee.

"I think I'll do the same," Griffith said and left.

"Me, too," Stallings left.

Harv looked at me. "Did you know Cross very well?"

"No. I only met him last night at dinner. Seemed like a nice guy."

"He was. He could be gruff, and I guess we all have had our run-ins with him, but I can't believe anyone in our group could have done this. We have all benefited from his management of the company."

"It didn't have to be someone that worked with him," I said.

"I've been with the company longer than Cross has. Nesbitt and I go back to the Hardzog era. A good guy and whew," Harv shook his head smiling, "what a ladies' man! But he's way too old now to step in."

"How about Geri?" I asked.

"She couldn't have done it," Harv almost smiled at the thought.

"No, I meant take over."

"Maybe. She was part of the management and profited the most from the success Cross brought to the company. Of course, she bought in and risked a boatload of her own money, so that's only fair. But all of us have seen our pay, bonuses, and other benefits go up every year since Cross took over."

"Do you have any thoughts on anyone outside your group having a motive to shoot Cross?"

"No, not at all," Harv responded.

"Well, hopefully the police will be able to figure it out."

"I pray they do," Harv said. He stood up and left the room.

"More coffee, sir?" One of the wait staff had approached me from behind, a pot of coffee in hand.

"Yes, please."

He looked like he might still be in his teens. He also looked a little nervous.

"Crazy morning, isn't it?" I asked.

"Scary is a better word for it," he said.

"Do you know what happened?" I asked.

"Only that one of the guests got murdered. I'm quitting this job once they say I can go. So is about half of the staff. We don't need this stress."

I took my coffee and walked out into the lobby. The police presence was still obvious, but the place had calmed down a little. I went out onto the front porch.

A woman in cowboy boots, black jeans, and a white ski jacket leaned against the railing. She had pulled her hood up over her head for warmth against the cold breeze. I contemplated getting my own jacket but decided it wasn't that cold and didn't plan to be out here that long.

A wisp of white smoke drifted by her head before a gust of wind blew it away from her. I couldn't see her face, but I saw the cigarette in her hand as it went back to the rail.

"It's peaceful out here," I said as I approached the railing next to her.

She turned and looked at me. "Jim," I sensed she was happy to see me. "How are you dealing with all the chaos?"

"A crazy day, Bev. Aren't you in early?"

"Rick called me. He said he needed the bar opened early today."

"Did he tell you what happened?"

She nodded, "This is going to be tough on Rick."

"Rick?"

"He's the general manager and also a minority owner. It's a family owned business. A lot of friction among the family members."

"Sounds like you know the family pretty well," I said.

"No, just Rick. He's a great guy. Only one fault," she said looking at me like I should know the punch line. "He's married. You're not married, are you, Jim?"

"No way," I said, playing her game.

"Good. Someday I need to break the habit."

"You'll let me know if I can help, won't you?"

"Where did you say you're from?" she asked.

"Clovis."

"Not too far away. I'll have to put you on my list."

"Bev," Rick called to her from the doorway.

"Hey, Rick," she walked hurriedly to him. "How are you doing?" She took one of his arms in her hands.

Some of the stress appeared to melt from his face.

"Oh thanks, babe. I appreciate your coming in to help," he said in a soft voice.

"Just what the doctor ordered," I thought. She followed him back into the lodge. The door had barely swung shut, when it opened again and Geri walked out of the lodge.

"Well, that was a waste of time," she remarked when she saw me. She took possession of the spot where Bev had been standing. I didn't see a cigarette, but I imagined seeing some smoke, which was more likely steam, rising from her head.

"What happened?"

"Really nothing, but that's just it. I explained that I knew nothing, nothing at all."

"That's all you could do," I said.

"I know, but they wouldn't tell me anything. They have to have some idea what happened to Cross, but they wouldn't tell me anything. Idiots! They wouldn't even tell me when we could leave."

"Give them a few more hours," I said. "It'll take them a while to get organized."

"Are you a cop?" she asked, some of the hostility still there.

"No, but I'm familiar with their procedures. Where's Vic?"

"Who knows?" She said it like "who cares," and I didn't think she did.

"Have you heard any more from Randi?" I asked.

"No. I imagine she's still sleeping."

"Do you know if anyone has contacted Cross' wife?" She shook her head. "This will be on the news fairly soon," I said.

"I need a drink," she said after a moment's silence.

"I think the bar will be opening soon."

"Hope so."

"Geri, Cross mentioned to me that this trip, the fall ones, don't include spouses--"

"They don't, except this year Vic wormed his way onto it when Fred had to cancel out at the last minute."

"Guess I can't blame him. Under normal circumstances this could have been a great trip for you all."

She looked at me with a puzzled expression and then looked away. "I hope they catch this guy and fast. None of this makes any sense."

"Well, I guess there's no reason why I would hear anything before you, but if I hear anything from the police about all this, I'll let you know."

She looked at me and smiled, "Thanks."

"No problem," I said. I wondered why I lied to people in times like this. A character flaw from the old days, no doubt. I might or might not tell her what I learned from the police.

"Who are you, Mr. West?"

"What do you mean?"

"I mean you're like an anomaly here at the lodge. You're by yourself--"

"Too easily explainable, unfortunately."

"More interesting, everyone else is either walking around in shock, or stressed out, or both. You, on the other hand, are as cool as the proverbial cucumber."

"Think I'm the murderer?"

"No. I don't sense that in you, but then why should I think I could?" She stared off at the trees.

"For the record, I didn't have anything to do with his death," I said.

"For the record, I didn't either." She gave me a halfhearted smile and walked back into the lodge.

I thought about staying on the porch a few minutes longer, but a gust of cold air convinced me to head back inside.

No one was at the bar, either in front or behind it. Two women on the hotel staff were comforting a female colleague who sat softly crying on a couch in the lobby. I looked into the deserted dining room. I placed my empty coffee cup on a table and went back to my room.

CHAPTER 7

By one o'clock, I had my fill of television and sitting around. I didn't feel hungry, but habit is a hard thing to break, so I headed back to the lodge's restaurant. Despite Geri's comments about my being so calm in the midst of all this, I felt the anxiety setting in. It bothered me that I hadn't been interviewed yet. I didn't like being held until last.

The dining room and bar were empty. In fact, other than one poor soul behind the registration counter, the whole place seemed abandoned. I walked to the hallway that led down to the crime scene. The police had taped off the end of the hall, and a lone deputy stood guard outside the room. I could hear sounds of activity coming from the room.

In the absence of anything better to do, I went outside and walked around the lodge until I was outside the window that belonged to the room in which Cross was shot. I looked at the ground below the window. Nothing seemed disturbed or gave me an indication that anyone had crawled in or out of that window in the past day. A normal person would have needed a ladder to access the window from the outside. The bottom of the window was about seven feet off the ground.

I decided to walk the rest of the way around the lodge. The backyard included a large, covered concrete patio with an immense brick barbeque pit set off to one side. A handful of metal tables with chairs sat on the patio, and a few benches were scattered around the lawn. A few tall pines had been left near the lodge. Further out the forest became thick. On a warmer day it would be pleasant out here, I thought.

I continued my trek around the lodge. All in all, my journey provided minimal exercise but nothing else. I didn't see anyone and didn't develop any clues or opinions on what had happened to Cross.

Two deputies walked out of the lodge as I went up the stairs onto the front porch. They ignored me as they walked by. I paused and watched them as they got into their old Crown Vic and backed up.

"Hey!" I shouted at them as they nicked the back bumper of my Mustang. They didn't hear me, or chose to ignore me and drove off.

I walked out and inspected my car. I was certain I saw the Mustang move slightly as the rear of their cruiser backed very close to my car. A small dark scratch looked new among the other older abrasions.

"Idiots!" The damage was minor, but it irritated me to think that they probably felt the slight bump and chose to ignore it. Too bad I didn't get a better look at their faces.

"Mr. West!"

I turned and saw a man whom I had not seen before standing at the lodge's entrance.

"Yes."

"If you've got a minute, I'd like to speak to you now."

"Sure."

He reached out and I shook his hand.

"I'm Detective Randall Bruno."

"Nice to meet you," I said out of habit.

"You look cold. Mind if we talk inside?"

"I'd prefer that, too."

"Follow me. They gave me a small office to use."

He looked nearly as old I was. His brown hair had some gray that he didn't try to hide. He had a slight paunch, but who didn't these days? His white shirt had enough wrinkles in it to make me think he might be single. Not that I expected all wives to iron their husband's shirts, but those who don't usually aren't too shy to point out that a shirt is wrinkled. I have also found that most men would be content if wrinkled clothes became stylish.

"Cup of coffee?" he asked when we were settled.

"No, I'm good."

"Do you mind if I call you Jim?"

"That's fine."

"Do you have any idea who may have shot Mr. Benson?"

"No."

"Did you know him well?"

"No, in fact I just met him last night at dinner."

"Did he mention anything to you that might indicate that he believed he was in danger?"

"No." I thought I was done answering the question, and Detective Bruno referred back to his notes rather than ask me anything additional. As he did so, I remembered something.

"He did make a fairly innocuous comment about still having to watch his back."

"What do you think he meant?"

"I don't know. I believe we were talking about his business more so than about his employees at that point. I didn't pay much attention to the comment at the time. Sorry."

"Did he talk much about the others?"

"Only that they were a good group of people."

"Any indication he was having trouble with any of them?"

"No, but like I said, I only met him last night."

"How do you get along with the rest of the group?"

"I don't really know them."

"But you were with them this morning."

"What do you mean?"

"After the shooting, you were with the hunting group in the dining room."

"It was either that or sit by myself a table or two away. I thought that might be awkward."

"But they let you join them?"

"Yes."

"And you carried Ms. Pearson to her room after she discovered the body--"

"If Ms. Pearson's first name is Randi, then I did."

"That doesn't seem like the act of a stranger. Weren't their others in the group right there?"

"Well, you've got me there, Detective. For whatever reason, Randi swooned against me--"

"You have that effect on all women, Jim?"

The question came across more like he was playing with me

than being caustic.

"I wish."

"What brought you to this hotel, and why are you alone?"

I liked this line of questioning better and for the next few minutes explained to him about Stu and how I got sucked into the trip.

"When were you planning to head back?"

"Tomorrow."

"Any chance I can talk you into staying at least a day longer?"

"Why?"

"I need someone who can be my eyes and ears on the inside?"

I looked at him but didn't speak. He finally started up again.

"Look, Jim, you're not part of his clique. You're not part of the staff. I also have it on fairly good authority that you were in the dining room when the murder took place."

"How's that?"

"The receptionist said that Benson asked if he could use an office right after you walked by him and headed into the dining room. The sales record in the dining room also sets the time the waiter started your order. It was one minute before Benson logged into the computer."

"You've done your homework."

"Not me, I've got some smart young kids on my team."

"Still, weren't most of the hunting group together down at the range?"

"Yes, but this whole case doesn't make any sense. All of

them could even be in it together."

"No weapon?"

"No, we haven't found the weapon. Other than staff, the only person that seems to have been floating around at the time of the murder was Ms. Pearson. However, piecing together what we have gotten from the staff, we believe she was in her room or in the lobby at the time Benson was shot."

"Have you interviewed her?"

"Just finished. We also ran a test for gunshot residue and searched her room. She was cooperative and said we could do anything we wanted, if it would help."

"Did she seem normal to you?" I asked.

"No less normal than most people I meet in this job. Why?"

"Nothing really, maybe I'm just getting old."

"Will you help us out? I know you've got a background in law enforcement, and I understand you have helped out in the past."

Damn internet. "It's not what I do. I didn't, well, it's not what I want to do." I knew he was referring to a couple of past misadventures I'd had in other murder investigations.

"But you did," he said. "So, how about this? You and I get together tomorrow morning at ten, back here in this room. Just talk to me one more time before you go. You don't need to do any snooping. I'm simply interested in what you might hear between now and then. Could you do that?"

"Fair enough," I said. He probably figured that I had to be as curious about the shooting as he would be if he was in my shoes. "What else can you tell me?"

"Like what?"

"Caliber of the weapon?"

"Small, likely a .22."

"No one saw anyone go into or out of the room?"

"No. Window was shut and locked and the emergency exit door at the end of the hall would have set off the alarm. The killer had to come and go down the hall to the lobby."

"Could he have gone into one of the rooms in the hallway?"

"Sure, but there are only a few, and all the windows in those rooms were locked from the inside. The only rooms that would have been easy to access would have been the rest rooms. The other two were locked."

"Someone could have been in the restroom, though, and emerged with the chaos of everyone running down the hall."

"Possible," Detective Bruno admitted.

"And someone from the staff could have accessed the locked rooms and come out in the same chaos."

"Again, possible. I don't need you to try to solve the case for us Jim. I just want some eyes and ears on the inside."

"What's happened to everyone's rifles and or other weapons?"

"There was some grumbling, but we took everyone's rifles under the pretext of eliminating them from the murder weapon."

"No one admitted to having a pistol?"

"No," he said.

"What was Cross doing in the room?"

"Something with fantasy football. I'm not sure of the details, but I can't imagine it has anything to do with his death. We've taken the computer though, just in case."

"How about the two guys that have disappeared?"

"The Bettes' boys?"

"Yeah."

"That's a good question. We've got a lot of people looking for them. Did you know them?"

"No, not at all. Do you know if they have any connection to Benson?"

"None that we know of."

We talked for a few more minutes before he let me go.

CHAPTER 8

When I left the interview, I saw Tom Griffith and Aaron Nesbitt head into the dining room. I went over and looked to see who else was there. A couple more of the hunting group sat at the same table they had chosen earlier, but Randi was not one of them. She had mentioned doing lunch together. I didn't feel much like eating, nor did I have a special desire to dine with Randi, but Bruno did get one thing right: I was extremely curious about what happened, and other than the killer, Randi knew more than anyone else.

Bev had opened the bar, so I headed there to wait for Randi to appear.

"Same thing?"

"Yes," I said, thinking she had a good memory. I took my wallet out of my pocket.

"No charge. Drinks are on the house for the rest of the day."

"Good thing I'm getting an early start."

Bev grinned.

"How's Rick doing? Handling it ok?" I asked.

"Touch and go."

I looked at her for more of an answer. She leaned in close.

"It's his sister. She's been gunning for his job ever since the lodge opened four years ago. Says he doesn't know how to make the place work."

"This didn't help."

"No. Somehow, she's making this out like it's his fault."

"Of course, it's not."

"I know it," she agreed, "but it's one more thing she's can use against him."

"Nice family."

"It's one of these rich, dysfunctional ones, although Rick claims she's the worst. Without her, he says the family would just have the normal squabbles."

"Heard any rumors as to who may have done it?" I asked.

"No. Must be one of the guests. There's some scuttle-butt that the two Steeler fans are connected with some murder around here in the past."

"You mean the two guys here last night in the Steelers sweatshirts?"

"Uh-huh," she nodded.

"How did you learn that?"

She smiled at me and hesitated.

"Let's just say an employee of the lodge has a close, personal relationship with one of the deputies."

"Interesting."

"Apparently it's got them all excited." She didn't elaborate on "them," but I knew she meant the Sheriff's office.

I thought about what she had said for a minute, and she came to the wrong conclusion.

"It's not me. I mean I've known a few cop types in my life, but I'm not the person the deputy spilled the beans to."

"I hope they catch them."

"Me, too. The quicker this mess gets resolved, the better."

"I'm surprised you don't have more customers. Free drinks are usually enough to draw a crowd."

"Free is one thing. Advertising the fact is something else," she laughed.

"Don't worry I won't tell," I said.

"Have you decided when you're leaving, Jim?"

"Tomorrow."

She didn't say anything, but she did take my glass back to the tap for a refill.

"How far away is this firing range the lodge has?"

"Oh, it's real close. It's just down the dirt road." She motioned with her hand at the far side of the lodge. I didn't notice a dirt road being close to the window of the room where Cross had been shot, but that was the end of the building she had indicated.

"An easy walk?"

"Maybe ten minutes. I'd take you, but I have to work. It's pleasant through the trees."

"Maybe I'll walk over there in a minute. I'll go stir crazy if I just in my room all day."

She broke open a large bag of pretzel mix and poured some into a bowl she had put on the counter next to us.

"I know I don't need these, but I'm hungry," she said.

We talked about nothing in particular over the next ten minutes. I declined another beer but did my best to empty the bowl before she could eat too much - I try to be helpful.

When I left to go outside, the bar area and the rest of the lobby were still empty. I retrieved my jacket first and took my car keys. Once outside, however, I decided to walk.

To be safe, I followed the dirt road. It might not be far away, but the woods around here can get really thick quick, and I didn't want to risk walking right by it and getting lost. It only took about ten minutes to reach the long, odd looking structure.

The road approached it at an angle and dead ended in a small dirt parking lot that fronted the building. The structure's outside walls appeared to be made of cinder blocks. The front consisted of a hardy board, or some similar product. The plain wood door stood ajar a few inches. A sign next to the door stated that the building belonged to the Royal Lodge and that trespassers would be prosecuted.

I pushed the door open and entered. In doing so, I nearly ran into a young Sheriff's deputy coming out.

"Excuse me," I said.

At the same time he asked, "What are you doing here?" He looked more nervous than I felt.

"Just getting a little exercise and I decided to take a look at the firing range," I said.

"Are you a guest at the hotel?" he asked.

"Yes, I'm Jim West." I instinctively held out my hand to shake his.

He held up his hand just high enough to show me he was wearing gloves. I pulled my hand back.

"What're you looking for?" I asked.

"Just checking the area out," he answered. He stood still blocking my entrance.

"Is there any reason this place would be off limits to me? I mean this isn't the crime scene, is it?"

He looked at me for a second longer before speaking.

"No, I guess not. Just make sure you turn off the lights and lock the door behind you when you leave."

"Sure, I'll only be here a second if you want someone to walk back with."

He grunted. "That's alright."

I eased by him and didn't watch him leave. I wouldn't have cared if he stayed and watched me, but he didn't. There was no need for him to keep an eye on me. The value of everything inside of the building, despite its size, had to be less than a hundred dollars. Other than the numerous fluorescent light fixtures, which had no real value, the only items a person could steal would have been plywood and two by fours.

A large plywood counter had been built across a large portion of the front wall. Nearby, a picnic table with bench extended a few feet from the side wall. I imagine this was where the range officer sat while individuals used the range. Several firing positions were framed on the ground by additional two by fours, and I do mean ground. The building had a dirt floor. A number of wooden crosses stood at different distances down the range. Two still had paper targets attached. The wall at the far end of the building was hidden by a high, dirt berm.

Just the basics, I thought. Practical, but certainly no frills. I didn't even see a restroom. Simple curiosity brought me here, but the deputy's presence made me wonder what he might have been looking for here in the building.

I glanced in the small trash can next to the door and saw a few paper coffee cups and napkins. Rather than reach into the trash can, I picked it up and shook it. I didn't see, or hear, anything else inside. The larger trash can by the picnic table was completely empty.

I walked the firing line looking for any discarded brass that hadn't been cleaned up. I found a few, but nothing small enough to be a twenty two. After looking around for nothing specific for another five minutes, I departed the building.

The trees hid the lodge from view for most of the walk back from the firing range. However, about sixty yards from where the winding dirt road met the lodge's parking lot, I came to a spot where the trees opened up enough to give me a very good view of the side of the lodge and of the window to the room where Cross had been found.

I studied the area and saw nothing of interest. Leaving the dirt road I walked directly toward the lodge and looked for any place that a shooter might have selected. There were too many to consider, and none of them looked disturbed. Not far from the road, I also realized that the ground had a slight slope to it. A shot from this position would have an upward angle. Anyone more than a few feet from the window would be impossible to hit.

I walked back toward the road. I had almost reached the road before I felt that a shooter would have an effective line to the target. From this distance, about thirty five yards, it would have taken a good shot, and there was still that problem with the physics. How to get the bullet through the window without breaking the glass?

CHAPTER 9

I followed the dirt road back to the parking lot. Two new sheriff's vehicles had pulled up to the very front. Their police lights were flashing brightly. I had no sooner wondered what was going on, when I saw two deputies walk out of the lodge with one of the Bettes' in handcuffs. He looked stunned, and I thought he might even collapse before they got him to their cruiser.

Right behind them walked the other Bettes, half consoling his brother and half yelling at Detective Bruno who had appeared in the doorway behind everyone. I stayed out of everybody's way.

The sheriff's vehicle sped away.

"Back inside!" Bruno barked at the remaining Bettes.

Bettes snapped back at him. I couldn't be sure what he said, but I didn't think it was something endearing. Despite what he said, Bettes followed Bruno inside. Once he cleared the doorway, a female deputy walked out, climbed into the other car with the flashing lights, and drove away. Three Sheriff's vehicles still kept their quiet vigil in the lot.

The excitement over, I entered the lodge wondering if the drinks would still be free. Once again, I discovered the bar empty except for Bev sitting off in a corner reading a magazine. A lone clerk behind the reception counter brought the total human population in the large open area to three counting me.

I walked over to Bev. She smiled and rose to meet me.

"You missed all the excitement."

"I guess I did. What happened?"

"Not too long after you left those two men walked into the lodge."

"And?"

"And…." she paused for effect, "two of the hunting group had just come out of the dining room. One of them looks back into the dining room and called to a deputy, who I guess was on his lunch break."

"What did he say?" I asked.

"Something like, 'Your two suspects are here.' The two men stopped dead in their tracks. They didn't say anything."

"Yeah. They don't talk much," I added.

"The deputy came right out and told the two to stay where they were. One of the two men asked what was up, and that's when one of the other men shouted, 'You murdered our friend!'"

"Ouch!"

"Between that remark and the deputy taking a step toward them, all hell broke loose."

"What do you mean?"

She grinned like she was enjoying the memory. "One of the two men bolted out the door."

"He just took off, like that?"

"Yep. The deputy shouted something and was out the door after him. Two or three more deputies came out of nowhere and raced out the door after them. The whole time the other guy stood there shouting at whoever would listen to let him be, that he hadn't done anything."

"Maybe he didn't, but running like that wasn't the smartest thing he could have done."

"They caught him after a few minutes, and by the time they had him cuffed and back in here, the lobby was packed with everyone. The deputy in charge finally had to yell at everyone and send them all back to their rooms."

"That explains why it looked like a ghost town when I came in."

"Yeah, there was quite a crowd here just a few minutes ago."

"Do you think he did it?" I asked.

"Could be, but his buddy was sure hollering in his defense. Apparently, the guy that took off has some emotional issues. At least that's what his buddy kept yelling."

"Well, hopefully they'll get to the bottom of it and things will soon get back to normal for you," I said.

"Except for the stress this is causing everyone, I kind of like all the excitement. Most of the time it's rather boring around here."

"I can't imagine life ever being boring for you, Bev."

She laughed. "I wish my life was more exciting. How about yours? I bet it's a lot more exciting than mine."

"I doubt it."

"What do you do, Jim?"

"Mostly nothing. I'm retired from the Air Force."

"You're too young to be doing nothing." She looked at me suspiciously.

At that moment, Detective Bruno and the remaining Bettes came out of a back room. Bettes walked off toward the stairs. He didn't look a bit too happy. Bruno looked over at me, nodded slightly, and walked out of the building.

"Looks like you two are buddies," Bev said. "You sure you're not some kind of cop?"

"Would you like me more if I was?" I joked.

"I told you I've been with a few cops in the past. Besides, I like you enough."

She looked up at the door, and I turned my head to see what caught her eye. Rick walked in and spotted us.

"Bev, what's the latest? I just passed that detective and he said things are happening. What does that mean?"

"Let me get this gentleman a beer, and I'll come talk to you in your office," she said. That seemed to satisfy him, and I soon found myself alone at the bar. I moved down to an untouched bowl of pretzel snacks and settled in.

I still had most of the beer and pretzels left when I saw Bettes, the one that had stayed at the lodge, approach the bar. He walked up to the counter and scanned the entire bar area. He looked like if he clenched his teeth any harder, his whole jaw would burst. I decided to be nice.

"Can I get you a drink?" I asked.

"You work here?"

"Not officially, but I bet if you want something simple, I can get it for you."

"I just want a beer." He looked at the choices on tap, "Sam Adams, preferably."

"Coming right up." I walked around the bar and poured

him a beer. After I set it in front of him, I walked back to my spot.

He smiled. "Who do I pay?"

"Don't you think they owe it to you after what just happened?"

"Yes. Maybe not the lodge, but the cops sure do."

"We'll put it on their tab."

"You can do that?"

"Sure."

"You a cop?"

"No. I'm just a guest like you."

"Not like me. I came here to help somebody, and everything's gone to hell in a hand basket."

"Sounds like my trip."

"What do you mean?" he asked.

I walked him through the reason for my presence at the lodge and my being stood up. While I talked, he guzzled down his beer. I picked up his empty glass and refilled it. I finished my story at the same time I returned with his beer.

"What's your story for being here?" I asked.

"It's too long and complicated," he said.

We sat in silence for a minute or two before Bev walked out of the nearby office. She looked over at Bettes' beer and then looked at me.

"Just put it on Detective Bruno's tab. He said it would be ok." I winked at her, and she played back.

"If you say so, but if he has any complaints, you can handle them."

Bettes laughed and said, "Let him complain to me." He

looked back at me. "What did you say your name was?"

"West, Jim West," I held out my hand, and he took it.

"I'm Colt Bettes. Let's move over to one of those tables, and I'll tell you what's going on. If you know Bruno, you may be able to help us."

I didn't comment on his remark, but I did follow him to a corner table.

"This is a long story, but you asked for it."

"No problem, I've got nowhere to go."

"Fifteen years ago, nearly to the day, my cousin, Sean, came out here for a vacation. He's always been an intense guy, so he had a habit of taking a week off and going somewhere by himself to unwind. Fifteen years ago, he came out here alone to hike and read."

"He certainly picked the right place."

"This place wasn't here back then. There were about a dozen rental cabins a couple miles from here. They're gone now. Razed and private homes built in their place. Well, two to three days into his trip out here something happened that has just about destroyed Sean's entire life."

"That's too bad," I said. I figured he might be exaggerating, "What happened?"

"I've gone through this so many times with Sean that I've started to feel as though it's my story."

"Are you his brother?"

"No, a cousin."

"That's right, you told me that, sorry."

"I happen to also be a psychologist. Sean has become a lifetime project, or perhaps I should recognize it as an obsession.

Unfortunately, it doesn't pay."

"I imagine he appreciates your help."

He nodded, "This trip was supposed to be the culmination of a lot of our work together. Now it's shot to hell in a hand basket."

An old phrase I hadn't heard in a while, and now I'd heard it twice in one day. "What happened to him back then?"

"The craziest thing," he paused for a minute like he was getting his thoughts in order. "It was just after dark, a few days into his trip. He heard a loud thud against his front door. He had been out earlier and while walking back to his cabin he had heard some strange sounds. His first thought was that some kids were simply trying to harass him, but when he opened the door a bloody body fell against him."

"A person?"

"Yeah, a woman, bloody and bruised as hell. Sean thought she was dead, but when he reached down to try to find a pulse, she grabbed him. Scared the crap out of him, and he blacked out."

"Who wouldn't?" I asked.

"That's only the start of the story. When he came to, she had moved away from him and had crawled into the cabin leaving a trail of blood. He followed the trail. It led into his bedroom. She had propped herself up into a sitting position on the floor with her back against the side of his bed. He had to walk around the end of the bed to get a good look at her. Once again he thought she might be dead. He approached her and knelt down. No way he was going to touch her again."

"Was she dead?"

"He says he had barely finished kneeling down when she opened her eyes and hissed at him."

"Hissed?"

"That's his word. He claims it wasn't a scream or a shriek or a cry. She hissed at him, raised her arm and pointed at him, and whispered something like, "You." Then she died. Her eyes still staring at him."

"That sounds like a horror movie."

"For him, I'm sure it was."

"What happened then?"

"Things went downhill."

"Downhill? How could things get worse?"

"Well, let's say it wasn't Sean's day. Terrified, Sean jumped up and ran out of the cabin. He would have probably run all night, gotten lost, and froze to death, if he hadn't run out of the cabin and across the dirt road right in front of a couple of deputies."

I could see where this was going. "They thought he did it?"

"Who wouldn't? They jumped out of their vehicle and shouted at him. Sean turned to them and started rambling about a dead woman in the cabin. He's standing there covered in her blood. When they inspect the cabin, it looks like she was dragged from the porch to the bedroom."

"You sure he didn't do it?"

"Not a doubt in my mind. By the time the investigation was over most the cops felt he was innocent. Never went to trial, but the days after the incident were just as hard on Sean as the incident itself."

"What do you mean?"

"Like I said, the cops' first reaction was to treat him like the killer. They interrogated him for hours right after the incident."

"He didn't ask for a lawyer?"

"No. Sean's remembrance of the police interrogation has always been hazy. I believe he was in shock throughout the entire ordeal. I know they kept sticking photos of the crime scene and the dead woman in his face and screamed at him to confess." Colt shook his head at the thought.

"What did they think was his motive?" I asked.

"They never had one for him. He was simply convenient."

A little more than that, I thought. He would be a logical suspect to anyone responding to the scene.

"He didn't get any sleep that night or the next day. I have no doubt if they had kept at him he would have confessed to anything."

"What happened to get him off the hook?"

"They got a lucky break that first day. It came in the same time they were still trying to break Sean."

"What was it?"

"The victim's concerned roommate called in to the police. She said the victim had called her late in the afternoon of the day of the incident and said she had a major row with her boyfriend. The victim told her roommate that she was afraid of her boyfriend."

"Did they check out the boyfriend?"

"Yeah. The roommate's description of the victim was dead on, excuse the pun. They had a bunch of priors on the boyfriend and knew he wasn't nice. I think at that point some of the cops started believing Sean's account. Anyway, late that day they put Sean in a cell to get some rest. There's even a side story there."

"That bad?" My mind shot to the worst of possibilities.

Colt must have guessed what I was thinking, "He didn't get raped or anything. Next cell to him they had just deposited a loud, angry drunk. Every time Sean dozed off, this idiot would start yelling and screaming to be let out. On top of everything else that happened to Sean, this was like some kind of torture."

It did remind me of a bad week of alleged training I had gone through as a cadet, many years ago.

"What happened with the dead girl's boyfriend?" I asked.

"They tracked him down in Santa Fe that night, but when the cops tried to pull him over, he sped off in his souped-up Chevy. They chased him for miles. Finally, he lost control on a turn and rolled his car about a dozen times. He died at the scene. They never got to interview him."

"Surely his fleeing from the police had to help Sean out."

"I think it did, but this guy had fled before, so some weren't too sure that his flight meant anything. However, they did let Sean go. In the middle of the night, by the way, but the damage was done. You ever hear of PTSD?"

"Yes, but that's usually in reference to wartime experiences."

"No, not at all. PTSD can be experienced by anyone who has gone through a significant trauma."

"I guess that's true. I just meant I've only ever heard it used before in reference to our war vets."

"Shell shock, battle fatigue, there's been a lot of terms for it, but the actual disorder does affect more than just the military."

"I believe it." I hadn't meant to challenge his expertise and certainly didn't want to get a whole lecture on the subject.

"Since that experience Sean's life slowly fell apart. He spent as much time as ever at the office, but his work became erratic. Before the incident, he could stay focused on whatever task they gave him at work. He got his projects done on time and with minimal errors. He was considered a valuable employee. After the incident, he lost his focus and his work suffered. The next time the company cut part of its workforce, they let Sean go."

"That's too bad. He's still not over it?"

"No, but these issues grow a life of their own. Being let go further affected his confidence and increased his anger at the whole world. He's held odd jobs since then, but a promising career had ended."

"When did you start working with him?"

"Shortly after the incident. His wife, ex-wife, called me within weeks of his return home. She asked me if I could talk to him." Colt shook his head again. "Talk to him. I wish it was just that easy."

"You boys look like you could use a refill." Bev dropped off two tall draft beers in front of us. "Bud Light and a Sam Adams, right?" She put a hand on my shoulder.

I looked at her inquisitively, about to ask how she figured out what I had poured Colt, but she spoke first.

"Want some chips or something?"

"Sure," I said. Bev turned and went to get the chips.

"You said ex-wife," I said to Bettes.

"Yeah. Sean had trouble sleeping, still does, but to a lesser degree. And, while I won't expand on it, the sex between them evaporated. His fault not hers."

"That's not good."

"No, never is. After a year or nearly two, she found another man who filled her needs – those are her words, not mine - better than Sean. She left him."

"Too bad," I said.

"You're divorced?" He must have inferred something from my comment.

"Yeah."

"How'd you take it?"

"Not good, but let's stick to your story."

"Sorry. It's a habit, but you can better understand the impact the divorce had on him than a lot of others can."

"Sure."

"Most people would think betrayal, or they might simply think slut, he's better off without her. But it's a lot deeper than that, isn't it?"

I figured he wasn't going to give me a free pass, so I decided to answer his questions but not give him anything additional. Sean's story wasn't mine, and I still wanted to hear the end of his story.

"Of course it is. I imagine he felt like he lost a part of himself when she left. I assume he was still in love with her?"

"In his mind, she was the anchor that held what was left of his life in place. Her departure devastated him. He tried to kill himself, twice."

"That's taking it serious."

"Individual's abilities to handle their emotions vary. Sean has a tougher time with his. Like I said, it's been a long time, and he's still in bad shape."

"Where were you today?"

"We went back to the site of the original incident, or at least what we think was the original location. The place has grown and private homes have taken the place of the rental cabins. Fortunately, the road is still there. Paved now, instead of dirt, but it follows the same route. The cabin stood near the end of the road. Nothing's there now. It's part of a larger lot."

"Any landmarks?"

"The old driveway, mostly overgrown but definitely a driveway at one time. The owners have left everything but a small area around the new house in its natural state. The house is set back off the road, probably centered on the lot. There was no fence and the owners did not appear to be home, so we just walked around."

"Did it do any good?"

"You never know; we talked about the event again, but we've done that a million times before."

"Ever done it out here before?" I asked.

"No. First time out here and my hope was that his seeing the trees, the mountains, driveway, whatever, would help bury the original memories of the place."

I wasn't sure how that was supposed to help, but then I wasn't the shrink.

"I don't mean to sound rude, but why are you here instead of with him?"

"I'm not a lawyer. They won't let me guide the interview, and besides, I think the guy in charge accepts our story. While Sean and I were out there we talked to a mailman. We also got gas at the country store. We used a credit card."

"He was shot early today. They may just think you went there afterwards to build an alibi."

"From what the detective said, I think we were getting gas about the time the guy was shot. Besides, we don't even know the victim."

"Well, I hope it works out for you both. Maybe the shock of this event will actually help him."

"I've thought about that. It's a possibility."

"Will they be bringing him back?"

"I doubt it. I agreed to meet the detective at the station at four. He said Sean would be released to me if nothing else came up."

"Detective Bruno appears to be a straight shooter."

"I don't trust cops," he said and finished his beer. "I need to go back to the room for a few minutes before I go." Colt stood up. "Thanks for the beers."

I watched him walk away.

CHAPTER 10

"You two looked like you were having a serious conversation," Bev said. She had walked up behind me as I was watching Colt leave.

"We were. By the way, how'd you know what he was drinking?"

"The Sam Adams? Easy, that tap drips for a while after every pour. I hadn't used it today, but I saw it dripping when I returned to the bar."

"Quite the detective," I said.

She smiled. Her smile looked genuine and warm. It could grow on me.

"I imagine he didn't say his brother was the murderer."

"No, he's actually his cousin, and I think I believe him. How long did you say you've lived here in this area?"

"Only a few years. Why?"

"His cousin went through a tough time about fifteen years ago. Seems like a woman came to visit him, just to bleed all over him and his cabin before dying."

"What?"

"You don't have a computer around here I could use? I think the internet might be able to explain it better than I can."

Bev went behind the bar and was back in seconds carrying an iPad.

"A modern woman," I said. I was only half kidding. I had stopped trying to stay up with technology when I retired from the Air Force.

"What are we looking for?" she asked.

"Look up Colt Bettes," I spelled his last name, "along with the word murder."

She started jabbing at the screen. She had chosen the seat to my right at the square table, but at the moment had the small tablet tilted toward her. I couldn't see what she pulled up. She tapped the screen a few more times.

"Jeez," she whispered to herself. She tapped the screen again. "Have you seen these?"

"No."

She started to turn the screen to me, but something else must have caught her eye. She touched the screen again.

"Take your time," I said.

"Did that guy tell you all about this?"

"Let me take a quick peek at what you've pulled up and I can answer that question."

"Oh, yeah," she turned the screen toward me. I leaned in to get a better look and she scooted her chair closer to the corner of the table.

"Man Implicated in Vicious Murder of Local Woman" ran the headline. Below the headline the article displayed a picture of a younger Sean Bettes.

"That's the story he told me about."

Bev read through the article and punched up another similar

one. "So, what did happen? The articles make it look like he did it."

I walked Bev through the story that Colt had told me. I left out Sean's emotional issues and what happened after that night. I figured his discovery of the dying woman on the front porch, passing out, and then finding her later in the bedroom made an interesting story by itself.

"Can you imagine?" she asked wide eyed when I finished. "I would have totally freaked out."

"Me, too."

Four of the hunting group strolled into the bar.

"Customers," Bev said. "I wondered when someone else would show up. Don't go away," she said.

While Bev walked to her place behind the bar, I studied the approaching four.

I recognized Aaron Nesbitt, the guy that looked like he had played professional ball, right away. I also recognized Harv but couldn't remember if someone had told me his last name. The other two I recognized as part of the group but had trouble fixing names with their faces.

I smiled and nodded as they passed by.   Only Harv acknowledged my presence. They ordered drinks at the bar and moved off to a far table. Bev carried a batch of mixed drinks to them before returning to join me.

"I have a feeling they're going to keep you busy," I said.

"That's good. I'd prefer to stay busy."

"You ever get any help here with the bar?"

"Sure, there're three of us. With the construction going on, however, one person can handle it. During peak seasons in the summer and the winter, we are busy with three here at the same time."

"I guess the lodge is lucky this didn't happen during a busy time."

"Yeah, not much business to disrupt at the moment," she said. "It's sort of like being in a ghost town around here right now."

"Speaking of ghosts, last night, two things happened to me that were kind of frightening."

"What?" she asked and moved in closer to hear my story.

"Well, first, after I had turned off all the lights and had just fallen asleep, my toilet flushed all by itself. I thought someone else must have been in the room with me."

"Oh, no!" she laughed out loud. "You got one of *those* rooms." She laughed again and smacked my arm. "They were supposed to have all those rooms fixed by now. Let the front desk know what happened."

"I take it that it's happened before?"

"Yeah, something to do with a slow leak in the tanks, or something like that. I thought they had fixed them all."

"Not mine," I said.

"In the past, some guests have insisted on being moved to a different room."

"I'm fine with the room, but I would like them to fix it."

"I'll take care of it," Bev said. She walked back to a phone behind the bar and talked to someone. After she hung up, she checked on the table of hunters before returning to me.

"Mission accomplished," she said. "Someone will be sent up shortly to fix the problem."

"Thanks."

"You mentioned that two things happened last night. What was the second?"

I smiled, thinking she wouldn't be able to come up with a quick fix for this story. "Later in the night, I heard someone crying--"

"Crying?"

"Sounded like a man. The strange thing is that it sounded like the person crying was above me, on the third floor."

"Where all the construction is going on?"

"Uh-huh. I thought it was strange, too, so I went up to investigate it."

"In the middle of the night?" She made a face of mock terror. "I would've called security."

"You have security?"

"Not really, but we're supposed to call management if we have a security issue. Tell me, what happened?"

"I went up and when I opened the door to the third floor and peered in, it sounded like someone left the floor from the other end of the building. It was too dark to see anything."

"Did you walk through the floor?"

"No, too dark and I couldn't find the light switch."

"Too scary, too. At least it would've been for me."

"That, too," I said with a smile.

She laughed. "That would've freaked me out. I never would've even gone to the third floor to look. Who do you think it was?"

"I have no idea. It sounded like a man."

"Weird. Why wouldn't he simply stay in his room to cry?"

"Maybe he was sharing a room with another guy."

"That's true. You guys can't bear to be seen crying. Uh-oh, they're waving at me."

I watched her go over to the group and then head to the bar. Another round, I imagined. I couldn't picture any of the guys in the hunting group being my crier. My money was on Sean. Colt said he had emotional issues. I debated with myself the value of asking him or Colt and came up with a draw. I would play it by ear.

"I'm sorry I missed lunch today."

I looked up and back at the voice. Randi stood right behind me dressed like anyone else might. Her hair this time was a very light brown. It looked like her natural color. She even had on normal clothing, jeans and a red blouse.

"That's okay. How are you doing?"

"Fine. This morning still doesn't seem real. I can't believe Cross is really dead."

"Sit down and join me, unless you're headed over there." I motioned with my head toward the foursome.

"I told them I'd join them. I'd rather sit with you, but I better go over there." Despite her comment, she didn't move.

"Did the police talk to you?" I asked.

"Yes. I think they think I had something to do with it."

"They probably wish it would be that easy. Did you confess?"

"No way," she said. "It'll take the third degree to get anything out of me." She grinned at her remark. "You're staying the night, right?"

"Yes."

"Good. Never know when a girl might get afraid again."
She winked and walked away.

"Your friend seems to have made a complete recovery," Bev
said when she returned a few minutes later.

"I was thinking that myself, but people don't always react to
things in the way we'd expect."

"True, but you will let me know tomorrow if she gets afraid
tonight, won't you?"

"Eavesdropping, huh?"

"What a good bartender does best," she said.

"I bet you hear a lot of good stories."

"I do, but I also hear a lot that I wish I didn't. You'd be
surprised how many customers would have their heads cut off
at my bar if they made me queen of the world."

"What do you mean?"

"One thing I've learned about men and booze, if they drink
enough, they brag about their conquests."

"Is that so bad?" I asked.

"Not necessarily. We girls do that too, but some of the
stories are horrid."

I didn't say anything, but I thought I knew where she might
be heading.

"If they made me queen, the next guy that bragged about
taking advantage of a subordinate who can't afford to lose her
job would have his head chopped off."

"Well, there are a lot of jackasses in the world."

"Yeah, and a lot of them don't need to be breathing," she said.

"Mr. Benson didn't happen to say anything that ticked you
off, did he?

She grinned. "Remember, I said I would chop off their heads, not shoot them."

"Just teasing," I said.

"Do you think they'll figure out who the killer is?"

"I imagine so. I think more murders get resolved than don't, but this one is a puzzler."

"What do you mean?" Bev asked.

"As far as I know, the murder weapon hasn't been found, no one has figured out the motive, and no one seems to have had access to the room but Randi--"

"That's your lady friend, right?"

"The one who was here a second ago, yes, but the police tested her for gunpowder residue and found none. She may be involved in some way, as any of them could, but I don't believe the police consider her the shooter."

"Too bad," she winked at me when she spoke and stood up. "I better get behind the bar before someone says something."

"I thought you had an in with the boss."

"An interesting way to put it, but I doubt if he would be very supportive of me if the complaint was that I was spending too much time with one of the male customers. That's another thing I would change if I was queen for a day. What's good for the goose would be good for the gander."

She walked back to her position behind the counter. She had grown on me since our first encounter.

CHAPTER 11

I finished my beer and went back to my room. I had talked more in the last two days than I usually do in a week. After kicking off my shoes, I ran through all twenty television channels. It's always amazed me that most hotels have a shorter list of channels than any basic cable or satellite option I've ever seen. Lucky for me, this one at least had the SyFy channel.

At a few minutes after six, I entered the dining room, and for the first time since my arrival, I found everyone already there. Not that everyone constituted a large crowd. Even Rick, the lodge's manager, sat at a corner table deep in discussion with Detective Bruno.

Sean Bettes had been released after all. He and Colt occupied the other corner table. The four looked like bookends, as each couple leaned in close together engrossed in their conversations.

The hunting group, at a table to my left, seemed to be somewhat agitated. Their voices were loud, and none of them appeared to care who heard them. I could see hands gesturing to emphasize feelings.

No one noticed my arrival, or if they did, they didn't

acknowledge my presence. Normally, I would've been grateful to be left alone; however, standing there, I had the irrational desire to be able to listen to any, if not all, of the ongoing conversations.

I grabbed the table in the center of the room. One of the wait staff must have been waiting for me to sit down. He stood ready to take my drink order as soon as I sat down. In Cross' honor, I stayed with the Heritage Oak wines. Besides, I liked them.

I had a good angle to study Sean's face. I thought I saw alligator tears and figured that he was most likely my night time crier. The guy definitely had issues.

The hunting group suddenly quieted down. The wait staff had arrived with their dinners. Randi looked normal, much as she did earlier in the afternoon. The rest all looked a little tipsy. Too much time at the bar, I bet.

I tried to compare the murder of Cross with other cases I had been involved in. The known facts matched an Agatha Christie mystery closer than anything I had seen before. How did someone get in and out of the room without being seen? How come no one heard the shot? What happened to the murder weapon? How did the murderer know that Benson would be in the room at that moment? At least the door to the room wasn't locked from the inside. That would be an Agatha Christie plot.

I had already assumed the murderer shot him at the same time the rest of the hunting group fired off their rounds at the nearby firing range. I thought one or two of the shots sounded different, but that would answer only one of the questions.

While any of a number of people may have known Benson would be in the room at the time, no one except the lodge clerk admitted to knowing it. The others in the hunting group knew he would be staying at the hotel, and he had mentioned to some that he needed to work on his Fantasy Football choices, but according to Detective Bruno none admitted to knowing specifically when he would be doing it or where.

If Randi shot him, a lot of the questions would be answered. But the police had talked to her and didn't suspect her, and I didn't think she was the shooter either. The gun powder residue test didn't implicate her, and what would she have done with the murder weapon? I suspected her swoon against me at the scene hadn't been totally genuine, but it matched her otherwise strange desire to flirt with me.

I wondered again about the lodge staff. Was someone new? Someone who had come to the lodge to work, because he or she wanted to be here when Benson arrived. A cleaning cart would be a perfect place to hide a pistol equipped with a silencer. A member of the staff could easily have gone into the room and shot him in the back of the head. Benson would have ignored someone who came into the room to empty the trash cans.

After the murder, the individual could toss the weapon under some dirty towels and stroll casually away. Perfect I thought, except if I remembered correctly, Detective Bruno had mentioned something about the staff all being accounted for at the approximate time of death.

A few of the maintenance crew had been allowed back up to the third floor. I didn't think they were part of the lodge's staff, but I also didn't think any of them had arrived before Cross was shot.

I remembered one old case that proved to be extremely

difficult to solve, until we did. It happened in Colorado, and started with a call by a woman claiming that her friend had been violently, sexually assaulted. Responding officers found the victim, a woman in her mid-thirties, in the basement of an empty house, where she had been discovered by her friend.

The victim had been dropped off earlier that day by her friend. They both worked for a cleaning service that got homes ready for sale or for the new buyers to move in. That day they were cleaning houses just a few blocks apart. Fortunately they both had keys to each house, so whoever got done first could go and help the other. They had a strict policy of locking the house while they were inside alone.

When the friend arrived at the house where the victim was working, she found the house locked. She entered the house and saw the victim's purse and jacket on a nearby chair. A portable radio played country music from a local station. The friend called the victim's name but got no response. She turned off the radio and tried again, still getting no response. She looked through all the rooms before heading to the basement.

She opened the basement door and saw that the basement was dark. She started to close the basement door when she heard a moan. She turned on the basement lights and was shocked by what she discovered. Four separate pools of blood connected by drops, smears and footprints decorated the otherwise drab concrete floor in bright red.

She heard the moan again and forced herself to go down the steps. She saw the victim sitting against a wall. Her jeans and underpants dangled from one leg. Blood was smeared over most of her body. Screaming all the way, the friend ran out of the house to a nearby neighbor. Together, they called the police and went back to investigate further.

They were still debating what to do when the first police officers reached the crime scene. Fortunately, they hadn't disturbed anything. By the time I had arrived, the victim had already been taken away in an ambulance. The initial prognosis was not good, but she did survive and fully recover.

At that scene we did have the locked door. Allegedly, there were only two keys to the house. We could find no sign of a break-in and nothing had been stolen out of the victim's purse. Despite the plethora of blood on the basement floor, the only bloody footprints we could find belonged to the victim. We finally wondered if the victim could have fallen and done the damage to herself. The basement door being shut and the lights to the basement being off seemed to negate that theory.

We knew our victim suffered a severe blow to the head. While she had other minor bruises, the blow to the head appeared to be the only significant trauma to her body. We found nothing in the basement that could have served as the weapon. The initial feedback from the hospital indicated she had not been sexually assaulted.

Our investigation changed focus as we tried to prove or disprove that this could have been an accident. We agreed it was possible, but not at all likely, that our victim may have tripped as she stepped onto the stairs. She would have had to pull the door shut behind her and either turned off the lights or failed to have ever turned them on.

Despite our doubts, we looked for anyplace she could have hit her head on the way down the stairs. Nothing jumped out at us, and the area around the base of the stairs was one of the few places in the basement where no blood stained the floor.

Our first inspection of the stairs revealed nothing, but a closer scrutiny of the area around the base of the stairs with the help of a bright flashlight disclosed a strand of hair and what looked like a tiny smear of bloody tissue on the screw end of a large bolt that protruded out of the bottom post supporting the hand rail. The bolt, along with one a few inches lower, fastened the bottom of the post to the side of the stairs. Only a few inches higher than the step next to it, it seemed impossible for our victim to have hit her head on it, but she had.

We figured she tumbled down the stairs, gaining momentum until her head crashed against the post. The blow to the head might have knocked her unconscious, and the bolt gouged into her skull at impact. Her hair blocked any immediate splatter and the speed of her fall pulled her head along with the rest of her body on past the bottom of the stairs.

Alone in the basement dazed, disoriented, and losing blood she had moved from spot to spot leaving pools of blood wherever she sat back down or collapsed. At one point she had the urge to go to the bathroom and instinctively had tried to remove her jeans. Her clothing revealed the corroborative evidence.

The woman recovered but never did recall what happened. She did remember going to check the basement, but other than looking down into the darkness, everything from that moment on was a blank.

I sat there, by myself, in the dining room sipping on another glass of an excellent zinfandel from the Heritage Oaks Winery, and wondered why that old investigation had popped into my mind. I didn't need reminding of what one of my old Colonel bosses used to drill into our heads, yet the case served as a perfect example.

He would encourage us, or antagonize us, depending on where you were on an investigation, by routinely reminding us that even the hardest puzzles look easier after they've been solved. He would chew up our theories and spit them back at us. He wanted proof or as close to it as we could get before we eliminated any possibilities. Many times, one of us would complain to whoever would listen that it made no sense to follow up further on something, only to have to embarrassingly admit later that we had missed something.

Something about Benson's murder didn't feel right. I knew it wasn't my case and that the Sheriff's office wouldn't want me second guessing them, but I had some questions and ideas I wanted to pass onto Detective Bruno.

"You okay?"

I glanced up, surprised that I hadn't noticed her approaching.

"Hi, Randi. How are you doing?"

"Too many drinks, but okay. I wanted to ask you to have dinner with me when I saw you in the bar, but I knew these guys wanted to talk business."

"With all that's happening, I guess I can't blame them." I noticed her face appeared a little flushed.

"Maybe so, but I'm tired of them all. This has been a bummer of a trip. I just want to get away. Can you take me somewhere, Jim?"

"Where do you want to go?" Better than saying, "I'd rather not" which is what I wanted to say.

"Anywhere, just away. Are you still leaving tomorrow?"

"Yes. At least I hope to. I have an appointment with the Detective sometime in the morning. I hope to leave after that."

"Maybe I'll come down to your room later tonight to talk. You wouldn't mind if I came down just to talk, would you?"

"No, not at all, but we could talk right now if you want."

She looked back at the group and for a moment I thought I saw a look of anxiety, or perhaps even fear, cross her face. "No, I'll come down tonight." She gave me a little half smile and walked back to the hunting group. Nobody seemed to be paying any attention to her.

By the time I finished my small steak and second glass of wine, I was alone in the dining room. I decided to have a third glass of wine and go for dessert.

CHAPTER 12

The hunting group had moved from the dining room back to the bar. They huddled in confidence at a couple of small tables they had brought together. At the far end of the bar, Bev looked like she was consoling Rick. His face stared down at the counter, and she slowly rubbed his forearm as she leaned in and talked to him. I decided to avoid them all and headed back to my room.

Too early to go to sleep, I turned on the television. An old James Bond movie I hadn't seen in the past year or two captured my attention for the next ninety minutes. After the movie, I went into the bathroom to shower and noticed a note from the maintenance staff telling me that they had addressed my complaint and for me to please let them know if I had any additional issues needing their attention.

While I climbed into my bed, I heard loud voices from the corridor. I couldn't resist the urge to move to the door and listen.

"...can't trust her. She probably did it!" I recognized the voice as belonging to one of the men in the hunting group, but not to which one.

"Listen! That kind of crap isn't going to get you anywhere.

Give her time.   Besides, the police aren't done looking into Cross' death. Who knows where a strategically placed tip will lead them?" This voice I thought I recognized. It belonged to Aaron Nesbitt.

"Ha! You ain't got the balls to cross her."

"Don't kid yourself. Now get some sleep, you're drunk," Nesbitt said.

I looked out the peep hole in the door but couldn't see anything. They sounded like they were in the hallway just a little to my right.

"I'm not drunk, and she just better be careful. She may have killed Cross, but I'm not afraid of her."

"I know you aren't. Now get in there and get some sleep. I'll wake you up in the morning for breakfast, okay?"

"Yeah, sure, don't forget me."

I heard a door shut then silence. No one crossed in front of my door, but that made sense as that direction would have only led to the stairwell that went to the third floor.

I used the room phone and called the bar.

"Bev, this is Jim. I need a favor."

"Well Jim, that sounds nice, but if you need room service I won't be off for a couple of hours."

"No, just some information."

"Oh," she sounded a little disappointed.

"Who has the room adjacent to mine?" I gave her my room number.

"You know we aren't supposed to release that information without permission."

"I know. I'll make it up to you," I said.

"It may not be safe being in debt to me, Jim."

"I'll risk it."

"Let's see, next door to you is a Thomas Griffith. Does that mean anything?"

"Yes, thanks. I owe you one."

"You do."

"Hey how's Rick doing? He looked stressed earlier."

"Not good, there's going to be a family meeting tomorrow."

"His job on the line?"

"He thinks so."

"Too bad."

"You should have come back to the bar."

"Why's that?" I asked.

"Had some fireworks a little while ago. Half the hunting group almost got into a fight with the other half."

"Oh yeah?"

"No hitting or pushing, but things got very vocal. Just when I thought it might come to blows, a couple of them got the rest calmed down."

"Well, I guess they're under a lot of stress right now, too."

"Who isn't?" she asked.

"Did the Bettes boys show back up at the bar?"

"No. I haven't seen them tonight. I thought the one was still with the cops."

"He's back. I saw him at dinner."

"Too bad."

"How come?"

"Well, if he was the murderer and had confessed a lot of this mess would be over."

"True, but I don't believe he's our murderer."

"You sure you don't want to come back down for a drink? No one's here now and I'm bored."

"Wish I could but I'm already in bed--"

"Hmmm."

"And I need to get up early tomorrow."

"Okay. I guess I'll see you tomorrow."

We said our goodbyes and hung up. I could only imagine what caused the fracas among the hunting group. Sooner or later, they had to realize that someone within the group had probably murdered Benson. While their initial anxiety likely focused on how Benson's death would impact each of them and the company, by now the probability that someone in their own group killed him had to be sinking in. That acknowledgement would spawn distrust and fear. Whatever bond they had before would begin to disintegrate.

I fell asleep dreaming that I was in the hunting group and that someone else in the group was following me everywhere I went. I kept looking around trying to find out who it was but could never see the person's face.

The door to the third floor closed with a bang and woke me. At least, I awoke thinking that happened. I shook my head and listened. Footsteps went by my door heading away from the stairway to the third floor, yet I didn't hear that door open or close.

My body cursed me as I forced it out of the bed and into the bathroom. I splashed cold water on my face and tried to wash off the hold sleep had over me. I put my jeans back on and went out into the hall. I saw no one and heard nothing out of the ordinary. Entering the stairwell to the third floor, I made sure the door closed quietly behind me. Nothing but the buzzing of an overhead fluorescent light broke the peace and quiet. I climbed the stairs and slowly opened the door to the third floor. If anyone remained up here I didn't want them to know of my presence. Although I had only seen a couple of workers during the day, all the ladders had been removed from the third floor corridor allowing me a better view down the still dark hallway.

The fumes from fresh paint irritated my eyes and nose. I was contemplating whether or not to walk to the other end when I heard a creaking sound. It took me only a second to guess what made it. Somewhere on this floor something heavy was hanging from a cord or rope and was gently swinging back and forth.

I started down the hall and noticed that all the doors to the rooms were open. The little bit of light that penetrated the windows provided just enough light to keep me from being in pitch black darkness. I peered into each room as I passed them. The ladders from the night before now stood in several of the rooms. The furniture in each room had been pushed into some convenient spot and covered with tarps. Window curtains and blinds had been removed. In a couple of the rooms, the ceiling had gaping holes where I imagined the maintenance crews were fixing areas damaged by water leaks or something else.

The sound, while never loud, became more noticeable the further down the hall I walked. I picked up my pace, and the hairs on the back of my neck started dancing. I had traveled about two thirds of the distance to the far end of the hallway before I came to the room. Unlike the others, the door to it was only open by a foot or two. I pushed the door to its full open position.

Even bracing myself for the unexpected, I felt the sudden intake of my breath and the adrenalin surge through me. I knew what was hanging in front of me, but I still reached for the light switch. Nothing happened. The light bulbs and fixtures had all been removed.

I wanted to run, to seek help, or maybe to just get away, but I didn't.

"Help!!" I yelled once, then again louder, while I ran the few steps to the body hanging from an exposed beam in the ceiling. Despite the darkness, I saw her face and recognized Randi. I felt her body. Still warm, maybe there was a chance. I grabbed at the chair that had been kicked over at her feet and stood on it next her gently swinging body.

"Help! Hurry!" I shouted again.

I grabbed her limp, naked body and lifted with all my strength. I fought to hold her high enough with one arm while I worked the noose with the other. I knew I could be destroying vital evidence if she was already dead, but her body was still warm and I couldn't be sure until I got her down to the floor.

The rope suddenly popped off her head and the momentum of my effort threw me off balance. I tried to hold onto the rope to keep us from falling, but the weight of our combined bodies along with my poor grip of the rope proved too much. We crashed as a tangled mess against the floor. A terrific pain shot through my right shoulder.

I forced myself to my knees and rolled Randi onto her back. I felt for a pulse, but my fingers were numb and shaking. I braced her neck with my hand and breathed into her mouth. I blew another breath again, harder this time, and moved to press on her chest. I pressed four or five times and went back to breathe for her again. I became dizzy but continued.

Somewhere in the back of my mind I kept thinking I had read about a new and improved CPR method. I felt like I was doing it wrong. She never responded to my efforts. I don't even recall who pulled me off her, but I remember being roughly pushed away and the room spinning in front of me. Lights erupted all around me. I closed my eyes and fought the urge to be sick.

I think seeing the words brought me back out of the fog of semi-consciousness. They stained the wall directly across from me.

"I'm sorry I had to kill him," written with what appeared to be a black magic marker stared me in the face. Below the words, neatly folded on the floor sat the clothes I had seen her wearing that evening. A magic marker rested on top of the folded clothing.

Two emergency technicians carried Randi out in a stretcher. A third technician, a short woman walked alongside the stretcher holding something connected to Randi.

"You feeling better now?"

I looked away from the gaggle with the stretcher leaving the room. A man I did not recognize squatted next to me. He had a small flashlight in his hand.

"Let me look in your eyes." He didn't wait for permission, but pointed the small light in one of my eyes and then the other.

I cringed and had to wipe the tears away, but tried to be a

good patient.

"How do you feel?"

"Okay," I don't know why I said it. My shoulder hurt and I felt horrible. If I were a few decades younger, I'd be calling for my mommy.

He stood up and walked off. I didn't watch him go, but before he left the room I heard him, "He's all yours."

That's when I noticed the deputy in the room with me. He looked young and frightened. I also heard voices in the hallway. I realized a lamp had been brought into the room to provide light.

I started to stand up.

"Stay down!" barked the deputy. "My orders are to keep everything just like I found them, and that includes you."

I didn't argue. My back and shoulder hurt when I tried to stand anyway, and I needed to get the last couple of cobwebs out of my mind.

"Is Detective Bruno on his way?" I asked.

He looked at me. I wondered if he thought telling me would violate some rule he had learned at his training academy. Finally, he came to a compromise answer.

"I'm not sure who is coming. I'm just following orders."

"I understand. Did you notice that?" I pointed at the wall.

He nodded.

"I don't think she did it," I said.

He took a step further into the room and studied the wall. He looked back at me. I could tell he was debating whether to speak or not. Finally his curiosity won out.

"What do you mean?"

"I don't think she killed Benson, and I don't think she tried to kill herself."

The deputy looked back at me. He didn't say anything.

"The lady they took out on the stretcher, was she alive?"

"I think so. You should know."

"I think I hyperventilated or something like that. I don't actually remember when everyone arrived."

He nodded but didn't say anything more. I heard people talking again in the hall. I thought I heard Geri's voice but couldn't be sure. The deputy momentarily glanced out the door to see what was going on. It must not have been Bruno, because everything returned to its quiet, peaceful state. Except for the rope hanging from a rafter, you might think nothing had happened in this room. That would change when the crime scene folks hit the room, and that happened after another three minutes of waiting.

Detective Bruno walked into the room with another deputy I remembered seeing earlier in the day.

"Everything the same as when you got here?" He asked the young deputy who had been guarding the room.

"Yes sir."

"Good. He said anything?" He nodded at me.

"Just that he didn't think it was a suicide."

"Hmm!" Bruno looked at me for a few seconds. "Go get yourself a cup of coffee, but stick around."

"Yes sir." The kid left.

"Did you see anyone up here with her?"

"No."

"Touch anything besides her?"

"Yeah. The chair, the light switch, the rope," I said.

"You got her off the rope?"

"Yeah. She was still warm and limp. I had no choice."

"Did she say anything to you?" He looked around the room when he asked this.

"No. She never regained consciousness."

"Too bad."

I didn't like the way that sounded.

"How is she?" I asked.

"Died before they got her to the hospital." His eyes focused on the clothing and the writing on the wall.

"Damn," I felt sick again.

He looked back at me. "You good enough to wait for me down in the dining room? We need to talk."

"Yeah."

"Okay, clear out. We've got work to do. Grab some coffee, I won't be that long."

An involuntary grimace escaped me when I stood up. Bruno noticed but didn't say anything. I walked out. I didn't rub my shoulder until I reached the hallway.

"Okay, guys. Come on in," Bruno called from behind me in the room. The half dozen members of the crime scene team streamed in after I was out.

Rick, the lodge manager and another young cop guarded the door to the stairs. They both stared at me suspiciously when I passed. I nodded at them, but they simply stared back. Once on the stairs, I rotated my arms at the shoulders. I had full mobility, but my right shoulder blade and back felt like they had been smacked with a two by four. At least, the tingling in my right hand had subsided.

The second floor looked like midday rather than after midnight. Harv, Stallings, Vic and Geri Schutte had gathered in the hallway and were engrossed in an animated conversation. They weren't being loud, but there certainly were a lot hands and arms moving around.   I had to pass them to get to the stairs.

They shut up when I got close, and each of them stared at me in suspicion.

"Not a good night," I said when I walked by.

None of them responded, however when I started down the stairs one of them whispered, "I bet he did it."

I didn't look back up. I saw both of the Bettes' sitting at a table in the bar, now closed. Sean had his head down in his hands. I heard Colt talking to him, but couldn't make out the words. He had placed his hand on Sean's right elbow. I imagined Sean's stress level had maxed out by now. A deputy stood guard at the front door. Bev had gone home long ago.

I returned to my room and stayed just long enough to freshen up and put on a real shirt. I hadn't needed to hurry. I had started a second cup of coffee in the dining room before Detective Bruno reappeared.

CHAPTER 13

"Okay, from the beginning West, tell me what happened tonight." He had a small notebook out in case I confessed.

"First, I need to tell you one thing that happened last night. It goes to my response tonight."

"You mean like twenty four hours ago?"

"Yes, give or take an hour."

"Go ahead."

"I heard what sounded like a man crying. It sounded like it came from the third floor. My room is on the second floor. I don't know how or why the sound penetrated to my room, but it did."

"So?"

"I went up to check it out, but after I got to the third floor, I couldn't hear it anymore. I did see someone leave at the far end of the hall."

"Who?" Bruno interrupted.

"Don't know. My view was hampered by the ladders and tarps in the hallway."

"Did you hear the crying again tonight?"

"No, and I actually don't think it had anything to do with

tonight's incident, except it increased my curiosity when I heard the creaking sound tonight."

"The what?"

"Tonight, around eleven, my noisy neighbors woke me up when they returned to their rooms. I got up briefly, and a little while later, after everything quieted down, I heard someone come out of the stairwell that leads up to third floor and walk by my door. I got up again and looked out my door. I thought it might be our crier."

"Did you see who it was?"

"No, but my curiosity took over, so I went up to the third floor. This time when I entered the third floor hallway, I heard the sound of the rope as it rubbed against the wood beam."

"You knew what it was?"

"No, but I had a feeling. I walked down the hall. The ladders and tarps had been moved so my vision to the other end of the corridor was unobstructed."

"Any lights on?"

"No, but the doors to all the rooms were open, and just enough light from the outside came in so I could see where I was going. I could also look into each room as I passed. I didn't see anything suspicious, and I kept getting closer to the sound."

"Could anyone have been hiding in one of the rooms you passed?"

"Absolutely. I kept walking until I got to the room where Randi was." I paused to see if he had another question. He didn't. "The door to the room, unlike the others, was only open a foot or two. When I pushed the door open I saw her hanging there."

"What else did you see at that moment?"

"The rope, the open section of the ceiling, and the chair. I didn't sense the presence of anyone else. I turned the light switch on, but of course all the fixtures and bulbs had been removed."

"Did you see the writing on the wall?"

"No, not then. I saw it later, along with the clothing, when she was being removed from the room."

He nodded.

"I ran to her and felt her skin. She didn't feel cold or even cool. All I could think of was to get her down and to try to revive her. Sorry if I messed up your evidence."

"You called for help?"

"Yes. I didn't have my cell phone with me, although I may not have even remembered that I had it, if I did. I just started calling for help. I set the chair back up. Someone had knocked it over."

"Someone?"

"She didn't hang herself--"

"We'll go there later. You set the chair back up and then?"

"I climbed up on it and lifted her up enough to work the rope loose. It took me a while, and when I finally succeeded we both tumbled off the chair."

"Your fall is what woke up half the hotel."

I ignored his comment. "Once we were down, I gave her CPR." I shook my head, "I'm not sure I was even doing it right."

"Don't be too hard on yourself. From what I've been told, you kept that little spark of life she had when you found her alive. The ambulance crew felt the same way when they took her from you. That there was a chance."

"Damn," I said. I also realized that I was now the one holding my head and looking down at the table. "I think Sean Bettes was the guy I heard crying last night. I don't think he had anything to do with this though."

"I'll need you to come back up with me and show us where you found the chair."

"Sure," I said.

"First, though, why don't you think this wasn't a suicide?"

"I just don't. Too much trouble to hang herself, plus I talked to her late yesterday afternoon, or maybe it was early evening. Anyway, she didn't sound like someone who was contemplating suicide. It doesn't smell right."

"Why would the killer fold up her clothes and then rest the marker on top of them?"

"To make it look like a suicide. I don't know. I just don't see it as a suicide."

"Despite the lack of evidence, she was number one on our list of Benson's possible murderers."

"I can accept her involvement in the murder and even possibly being the murderer."

"That's grand of you," he said.

"I don't mean it that way."

"Did you know her before this trip?" he asked.

"No, and I have no motive at all to do her any harm."

"She did seem to have an attraction to you."

"It's a curse," I said half joking. My reference related to people dying around me since I left the military, not women falling for me. However, I didn't think elaborating would be in my best interest.

"Anything else you can think of that I should know?"

"No," I answered honestly.

He led me back up to the third floor. We took the elevator, this time. Once there, I showed him the earlier position of the door and put the chair back to where it had been.

"Anything else?" he asked again.

"No."

"I still want to talk to you in the morning. We may have to move the time around a little, but don't go anywhere before we meet."

"I'll be here," I said and went back to my room.

The message light was flashing on my room phone. I listened to the message.

"Jim, this is Bev. I heard that woman killed herself tonight, and you found her. Are you okay? Did she really kill herself? I feel awful for you. I just wanted to make sure you're okay. If you need to talk to someone, give me a call. My number is 555-6084. Don't worry about the time. Bye."

That woman? Of course she knew her as the woman who came by to talk to me earlier in the bar. She had teased me about her.

I didn't call Bev back. I would see her later. However sleep, my number one priority at the moment, eluded me. Instead, my mind raced with a million competing thoughts. Most of them didn't even make sense. Should I have noticed something else in the hall? In the room? Did I, and did it simply slip from my mind? Did the killer see me?

When sleep came, things only got worse. I was back in the room trying to get the noose off Randi. It wouldn't come off and she was crying, "Hurry, hurry." It wouldn't come off. I woke up in a sweat. I slept again, and again I was back in the room. This time I got the rope off but rather than breathe into her, I was kissing her and she was kissing me back. Then, in my dream, I suddenly realized she wasn't kissing me. I saw her vacant, dead eyes, inches from mine, staring at me. I awoke with a gasp.

I had a desire to get up, read, and escape the nightmares, but stayed in bed and tried to focus my thoughts on happier things. It didn't work, but at least my dreams didn't wake me again before morning. I remembered that last disturbing dream though. In it I was performing CPR vigorously on Randi, trying to keep her alive. A doctor pulled me away from her and snarled at me. "You fool! Her heart is not on that side of the chest! You killed her! You killed her!"

Needless to say, I think I felt more tired at seven thirty in the morning than I had when I went to bed a few hours earlier.

Randi's death troubled me a lot more than Cross Benson's. Obviously, my being there had made it personal, but there was more to it than that. Both individuals had befriended me, but Randi's strangeness had both intrigued and bothered me. While the police may have to peel back Benson's personality and past to solve their crime, I had no interest in what made Benson tick. My mere presence at the lodge during Benson's murder brought about my interest in analyzing it. I would be happy to go home at any time and leave it to the police.

On the other hand, the same behavior in Randi that had the

contradictory impact on me before now served as kindling to the small fire of curiosity that had started to burn inside of me. Randi's death inexplicably created a personal desire to understand what had happened.

CHAPTER 14

"How're you feeling this morning?" Detective Bruno asked me as I munched on a piece of toast.

"Not well, but I'm okay. How about you? Did you get any sleep?"

"A couple of hours."

He must have slept here, I thought, as he had on the same shirt with a bleach stained collar that he had on the night before. Plus, he hadn't shaved.

"Let's go over again what happened last night."

I gave him a look that indicated I really didn't want to do that, but he ignored me and waited for me to start talking. Over the next fifteen minutes I covered everything. He seemed satisfied.

"Why do you think it wasn't a suicide?" he asked.

"My gut, mainly."

"Did you know that she had tried to commit suicide twice before?"

"No. When?"

"Admittedly the last time was nearly twenty years ago, but there is a history."

"How did she try to kill herself back then?"

"Pills one time, slashed her wrist the second time."

"Real attempts at suicide, or gestures?" I asked.

"Real enough that she needed medical attention."

"Still, that doesn't change how I feel. We had a couple of short conversations the last two days. Yesterday, I had the feeling she wanted to tell me something. I got the impression something frightened her."

"I heard she may have had more than a casual interest in you," he said. His face told me more than his words.

"I don't know what she had for me," I responded. "I couldn't read her that well. However, I didn't get any feeling at all that she was despondent enough to commit suicide."

"What had she said to you?"

"Her comments were always accompanied with sexual innuendo, but she did say she wanted to talk to me. I think she saw me as a safety base away from her group. Benson, in a conversation we had at dinner that night, alluded that Randi might come across as being easy, but that I might have better luck elsewhere."

"You mean with the other woman?"

"Yes, but that's why I kept thinking Randi's remarks signaled more of a need to get away from the hunting group and talk to someone else. That someone else she picked was me. Only, we never got to talk."

"Too bad."

"Yeah," I looked over at a handful of the hunting group. They huddled together at the far end of the room, but every now and then one of them would peer in my direction. "One other thing, when she mentioned she might come down to see me in my room last night, I thought I saw a look of fear or apprehension. I may have been mistaken."

"Yeah, you mentioned that. You might not be wrong." He glanced over at the hunting group and back at me. "Listen West. If it wasn't for the fact that you were trying so hard to keep her alive last night, and the fact that I've been doing a little checking on you, you would be on our prime suspect list."

"I didn't do it, Detective."

"I believe you," he looked over at the hunting group again, "but they don't."

"I can't say as I blame them. I'm an outsider. They know I was inside the lodge when Benson was shot and with Randi up in the room where she died."

"Should I take you in?" he asked smiling. I didn't respond to what I hoped was his joke.

"Women don't usually commit suicide by hanging themselves, do they?" I asked.

"You'd be surprised. Maybe not as often as men, but I don't think there's that much of a difference. The folding of the clothing is a woman's thing though. I've never heard of a man doing it."

"Would a woman get naked simply to hang herself? Why expose herself like that?"

"Good question, but I can't see a man doing it either."

"True," I acknowledged. "Seems overplayed, something a killer might want to do to play games with us."

"Could be."

"Randi wasn't very tall. Average height, maybe five foot

four or five. Even on a chair getting that rope over the rafter and securing it would have been a hassle."

"Would have been a hassle for a couple of the guys, too," Detective Bruno said.

"Well they're all taller than she was. The tall guy, Nesbitt, wouldn't have had much trouble, and a couple of the others - Vic, I can't think of his last name at the minute—"

"Schutte."

"Yeah, Geri's husband and Griffith are both tall enough to make it relatively simple," I said.

"If simple was important."

"You have me rambling. Does this mean that you don't think it was a suicide either?"

"Just looking at all the possibilities," he answered. No doubt he knew a lot more than he was sharing with me.

"She could have been involved in Benson's murder," I said.

"I would bet she was, but unfortunately, she won't be able to confirm it now. That note had to be written as either a confession by her or written by the true killer to mislead us."

I felt like saying, "obviously," but refrained.

"I imagine you're right. Still, though, even if she didn't shoot Benson, she may have known something about the murder that the killer didn't want her to be able to tell anyone."

"I assume you searched her room again," I said it rather than asked it.

"Of course. There was nothing new. But get this, her friend, Mrs. Schutte, spent the night with her in her room. Somehow, we believe, she, and not Randi, took the Xanax provided to Randi to help her sleep."

"Now that's interesting."

"We had a hell of a time waking her up last night to interview her. She's adamant she didn't take it on purpose and has no idea how it would have gotten into her system."

"Believe her?"

"At this point, I do. She carried around one of those Arizona ice teas for about two hours. Our guess is that someone drugged her drink. She claimed to have finished it when she and Randi turned off the lights to go to sleep, around eleven thirty."

"Where was the medicine kept?" I asked.

"On the bathroom counter in the victim's room."

"Could Randi have doped her?"

"She doesn't remember Randi ever getting close to her drink. She thinks someone must have slipped it into her drink when everyone, except Randi, was in her room after dinner."

"Could you tell if an extra dosage or two were missing?"

He smiled. "I heard you were good." I didn't ask him who he had been talking to. "We did. From what we can tell the prescribed amount was missing, no more. We'll do lab tests on the victim, of course, but she may not have taken her nightly dose."

"An absence of it in her system may imply she wanted to stay awake. Maybe to meet someone?"

"Or to hang herself," Detective Bruno added.

"But we don't believe that do we?"

"Between you and me?"

"Yeah."

"No we don't."

"Good."

"What did you hear from or learn from the others yesterday?"

"Nothing much. The team was starting to fall apart. Now, I imagine there will be too much suspicion and distrust for them to ever work together again."

He pressed me further. I didn't have anything to give him, but I couldn't blame him for pushing. They needed a break, and it wouldn't have been the first time a witness knew more than he thought he did. It would've made me happy to suddenly remember that golden nugget of information, but it simply wasn't there.

"How long are you going to be able to keep people here?" I asked.

"Not much longer, I'm afraid. Another day, possibly two, but if we don't come up with a strong reason to keep them here, I'm afraid everyone will be gone by tomorrow night, Monday morning at the latest."

"I plan on leaving tomorrow," I said matter-of-factly.

He didn't object, nor did he seem pleased by my remark. We talked a little longer about nothing before we departed company.

I went out front onto the porch. The sunshine beat through the thin high atmosphere and felt warm against the cool air. It should be a beautiful day. I contemplated taking that hike I came up here to do. A faint smell of smoke was in the air.

I returned to my room and put on my walking shoes and a sweatshirt. The sun might be warm, but in the shade of the forest I knew it would still be cool. I opened the bedroom window. I think I did it out of curiosity to see if the smoke smell was still there. The window screen prevented me from leaning out and looking around. I closed the window and in doing so, I realized something that I should've have noticed before.

The thought of a distant forest fire left my mind, and I immediately headed down to find Detective Bruno. He stood, leaning against the front registration desk, and talking to another detective.

"You got a second?" I asked.

"Sure. What's up?"

"I have an idea. Bear with me for a second."

He followed me while I led him to the room in which Benson was shot. The other deputy came with us.

"Good," I said to myself after walking into the room. I turned to the two detectives. "This may just be one of those anomalies that may or may not be significant, but it is something that is not what it is supposed to be."

"You're not making sense, West. What are you talking about?"

"What do you see?" I pointed to the lone window in the room.

"A window," the other deputy answered somewhat sarcastically.

"Anything else?"

Both walked up to the window and studied it more closely.

"You win," Detective Bruno said to me.

"Where's the screen?"

He looked back at the window. I could also see a light

turning on in his mind.

"What makes you think there ever was a screen here?" the other deputy asked.

"There may not have been," I said, "but I know most of the windows here at the lodge have screens."

"Which means someone could have opened the window to allow Benson to be shot from the outside. They would then only have to close the window before anyone noticed it had been opened. Anyone could have closed that window during all the early panic and commotion and not have been noticed."

I nodded at him.

"Then where's the screen?" asked the skeptic.

Detective Bruno turned on him. "Why don't you go find out, Jack?"

He left without saying anything else.

"I'm surprised no one noticed it missing before."

"An easy thing to overlook," I said. "Missing things frequently are, and none of us had been in here before yesterday."

"True." He opened the window and looked around outside. "We've already canvassed the area out there. He must have hid it."

Bruno brought his head back in, and I stuck mine out. Jack was just rounding the corner. He saw me.

"Is Detective Bruno still there?"

"Yes," I backed away from the window and let the detective assume the position.

"The clerk at the front desk said he thought there was a screen on this window. He's double checking with maintenance," Deputy Jack sounded like he was finally getting excited about my theory.

Bruno grabbed his phone. "Steve, get a couple more deputies out here ASAP." He listened for a second before speaking again. "I know we're not the only thing going on, but everyone here is tied up right now with the second incident, and I need something followed up on pertaining to the first incident."

He grunted into the phone a few more times before hanging up.

"Jack, we already scoured this area. Look out around the perimeter, especially behind the lodge."

"You know, it may not mean anything," I said.

"I know, but it's the first lead we've had since the interviews yesterday morning."

I knew that wouldn't be true. They had to have a million background leads being conducted down in El Paso and perhaps elsewhere. Here at the lodge, however, it did give them something to pursue.

"She could've shot him, opened the window, and tossed the gun to an accomplice," he suggested.

"But she didn't have any gunpowder residue on her. More likely, she simply closed the window for the shooter before she started screaming for help."

"Either way, it's too bad we won't be able to ask her."

I nodded.

"If we find the screen we can look for prints, but that's a long, long shot."

"Finding the screen?" I asked.

"Partly, but mostly finding any useful prints."

"Do you know if anyone else had access to this room earlier in the day?"

"The lodge staff uses this room for some of their own business, but also allows guests to use it. There's not a separate business office or computer room set aside for the guests, so this is it. They don't keep a record of which guests use it."

"Can you get that from the computer?" I noticed the computer had been removed.

"We're looking into that now, but that would only identify anyone who used the computer and signed into some site that would help us with identification. Anyone could have come in here just to scope out the room."

"And open the window," I added.

"Yep," he said. "We already know a couple of the guests had been down here."

"From the computer?"

"No. From the interviews."

Rick, the hotel manager, stuck his head in the door. "Detective, I understand you had a question about this room?"

"Do you know where the screen is for this window?"

Rick walked over and studied the window. I don't know if he thought he would be able to see the screen while we couldn't or what. He looked pale.

"The screen?" Detective Bruno asked again.

"It should be there. We checked with maintenance. All the window screens should be in place and in good shape."

"Do you know when the one for this window was last seen?" Bruno asked.

"Not for sure, but after the second floor was finished last weekend, I asked maintenance to do a thorough inspection of the first floor to see if anything needed touching up before we moved the contractors to the third floor. We had the first floor touched up last year, and I wanted to know if there were any odd jobs on this floor that might be too much for our lodge maintenance staff."

"And someone saw the screen then?" I asked.

"I can't guarantee it, but windows were specifically on the checklist used during that inspection. Nothing about that window was noted, so maintenance believes it must have been there then. I think it would have been noticed if it was missing."

"Thanks," Bruno said.

Rick looked at both of us and realizing that he had been dismissed, left the room.

"I hope I don't look that stressed out," he said after Rick was out of sight.

"I understand that all this may cost him his job."

"I thought his family owned the place."

"True, but apparently he has other siblings who think they can run it better," I said.

"I wouldn't want to run a hotel. You could never keep everyone happy, and there is always someone who wants to complain."

"Well, at least we know that the screen should have been there."

The detective looked out the window for a moment and then turned to look at the desk where Benson had been sitting. He squatted down to get a line of sight for someone shooting into the room.

"He would have to take the shot from somewhere in the tree line."

"Actually nearer to the dirt road that leads to the firing range," I said.

He looked at me. I would've liked to have said he was impressed, but I figured it was actually suspicion.

"I was bored yesterday, so I went out there to see where someone would have to be situated in order to get a good shot at Benson. You would have done the same thing if you weren't so busy with everything."

"Why didn't you say anything earlier?"

"At that point, it was an unlikely theory and Randi was still alive. Additionally, the missing screen had not entered my mind."

"Well if you come up with any other stupid theories, share them." His phone rang again and he talked to someone for a few seconds. "I have to go meet the new arrivals. Don't go anywhere today." He left me alone in the crime scene.

I walked around the room. I studied it and imagined Benson sitting at the desk. I thought about Randi coming in, seeing Benson slumped over, and calmly going to the window and closing it. Could she have done it? Was she that cold? Why would she have helped someone else kill her boss?

"What are you doing here?"

I turned and saw a young deputy I had seen once or twice before in the lodge.

"This is a restricted crime scene," he said with authority.

"Detective Bruno was here with me a few minutes ago. He gave me access."

The deputy eyed me suspiciously. "Well, you better leave now."

I ducked under the police tape and went back to my room.

CHAPTER 15

I didn't stay in my room for long. I had too much on my mind. Not too sure what I wanted to do, I grabbed my jacket and went out to my car. I got in and considered driving over to Glorietta. I knew it wasn't too far away, and I thought the trip might clear my mind.

One of the better memories of my high school years took place there. I went to Glorietta with the church youth group. One of the other group members was also a high school junior who I thought was one of the foxiest brunettes I'd ever known. Reflecting back, even with the many more years behind me, and after meeting many more brunettes, I still think she may have been.

Up to that point, we had just been acquaintances. By the time we left, we were an item. It lasted about a semester, ending when her family moved to Artesia with the oil business. I hadn't seen her since.

I had put the keys in the ignition but hadn't turned my car on yet. As I began to turn my keys in the ignition, I saw Sean Bettes walk out of the lodge. He seemed to be in a hurry and almost jogged across the front of the building, disappearing around the side of the lodge.

If he had gone toward the other end of the lodge I might have driven away. But the dilemma of the missing screen had its hooks in me. I climbed out of my Mustang and started after him. By the time I rounded the corner he had disappeared. I figured he had gone behind the lodge.

I cut through the side yard. Off to my right I could see a deputy walking around in the trees. I wondered if he was looking for the missing screen or for the place where someone may have positioned themselves to take the shot at Benson. Once I was behind the lodge, I noticed another deputy scouring an area of heavy shrubbery just beyond the tree line. I still couldn't see any sign of Bettes.

A well-worn path led from the lawn into the forest. I followed it and passed within a few yards of the deputy, who looked up at me.

"If you're looking for your friend he went by here less than a minute ago," he said.

"Oh, thanks," I responded.

"You might want to walk a little faster, mister. He was quick timing it."

"Thanks," I said again. "Quick timing," now that was a term I hadn't heard in a while. I figured the deputy had a military background since the only time I had ever heard that term used was when I was a cadet. It referred to a fast paced march.

Well, I had wanted to hike through the forest, so I guess this was going to be my opportunity. I picked up my pace a little. I didn't need to catch up with him if he never stopped. I was more interested if he stopped somewhere.

I actually suspected that he would not stop, but turn around at some point, and I would run into him on his return to the lodge. I wouldn't have bet a nickel that he was involved with either death, but I was still curious.

The trees blocked enough of the sun's rays to keep the chill in the air, but soon the path took on an upward slope and the exertion warmed me. The thin air smelled of pine. Every now and then I came to a clearing and was amazed with the beauty of the scenery around me. Large Douglas firs and pinyon pines towered over everything but the distant mountains that seemed to surround me out here. A few aspens added color and variety to the landscape. The further I got from the lodge, the less I cared whether I ran into Bettes or not. Besides, he wouldn't have discarded the screen this far away from the lodge.

My cell phone clock indicated I had been walking about twenty minutes when the terrain became very rugged. The ground changed from soft dirt covered with centuries of pine needles to rock or thinly covered rock. I walked another five minutes, climbing up and down a series of small gorges. I knew I could use the exercise, but this was no longer fun. Maybe the effort would be good for Bettes, but I'd had enough. I turned around and in doing so caught a glimpse of someone standing on the precipice of a small cliff.

Despite the distance of about a hundred yards from the path, I recognized Bettes immediately.

"Oh, come on," I said to myself, in more of a groan than a statement. Rather than start walking back to the lodge, I cut diagonally across the rough terrain toward Bettes. I contemplated shouting at him from this distance but couldn't decide whether that would just spook him into jumping.

I didn't need to be around another person dying – ever. I stumbled over some loose rocks and fell. My right knee took a direct hit on a larger rock and the impact reignited the pain in my right shoulder. I stood up cursing at myself and continued toward Bettes.

"I don't know if you're up high enough to effectively do the job," I said to him from about twenty yards.

He turned toward me and then looked down. From where I was I couldn't see over the ledge. I walked closer to him.

"I appreciate your concern, and I'd be lying if I said the thought of jumping hadn't crossed my mind. However, I didn't come out here to kill myself."

"Oh. In that case, sorry. So then why the long pose at the edge of a cliff?"

"Come look," he said and stepped away from the ledge.

Heights don't necessarily scare me, but for whatever reason walking by Sean Bettes to the ledge sent shivers up my spine. A slight gust of cold wind struck me at the same time and enhanced the effect. I peered over, my eyes searching for whatever he wanted me to see below, my ears listening for any movement from behind.

I didn't hear anything behind me. I glanced back at him. He didn't look like he had any intention of pushing me over the cliff, so I looked again at the ground below.

"See it?" he asked.

"Oooh! The dead elk?"

"Yes."

It looked pitiful to me and disgusting. While I'm in no way an expert on elk, this one looked very large and old. I had no idea how the elk had died, but since its death nature's scavengers had done their thing. The elk's front half appeared to be mostly intact, but the back portion had been ripped open and now appeared hollow.

"Not a pleasant sight, I know," Sean said. I realized he had moved up next to me. So much for my ears.

"So why the fascination?"

"It's complicated," he said.

"Must have been a grand animal in his prime."

"Weren't we all?" He said it without emotion, but I figured deep underneath, the tone was covered with self-pity.

"Don't I know," I said without knowing why.

He looked at me. "I guess that poor creature reminds me of myself. Half there and half eaten away."

"Except he's dead."

"Perhaps, I …." He paused for a second, "I'm sorry, I don't need to bore you."

I didn't say anything to encourage him to change his mind.

"You know, I was the first one that got to you last night."

I studied his face for the first time. His eyes had the look of someone who had been beaten down too many times to have any fight left. I'd seen it before in the eyes of some refugees who had lost everything and suffered continued abuse in the camps. I hadn't seen it on many Americans.

"I don't remember that."

"You were too busy trying to keep that poor woman alive."

I nodded in acknowledgement, and then looked back down at the elk. "Pitiful thing," I said and realized I was now shaking my head. I also realized I was talking about Randi, not the elk.

"Did you see anyone else up on the third floor?"

"No," he answered, "the cops asked me the same thing. There was no one else there."

"I didn't see anyone either."

"I couldn't stay and help," he said. "I should have, I know, but I simply ran downstairs and called for help."

"That was just as important."

"No, but it did get things moving. I guess I was coherent enough. One of the clerks called 911 and another one ran back upstairs with me."

"You're too hard on yourself. Getting the ambulance there was the most critical thing that needed to get done."

"He offered to help you, but you just kept at it."

"I don't remember that either."

He paused for a moment before saying anything else. I wondered if he was deciding whether to believe me or not.

"They had to pull you away from her."

"I do remember that."

"Do you think you could have saved her?"

"I tried. If I were a doctor maybe I would've known to do something different." After I answered, I wondered why he asked me such a direct question.

"Do you think you could've saved that lady? The one that came to your cabin long ago," I asked.

He studied my face. I looked at his. No shock or surprise there.

"I could've tried. I should've tried."

"You would've Sean, but the shock of it all affected you. There's nothing shameful or wrong in that. Your body reacted on its own, in probably the same way the majority of people in the same situation would have reacted."

"I returned to the third floor last night with the guy from the lodge," he repeated. "I watched you try. You were almost frantic in your efforts. I thought that there was no way you were going to let her slip away, but she still died."

I wondered what he was getting at. I didn't think he meant anything disparaging by his comments. He spoke softly, like he intended the remarks for himself as much as for me.

"It's not always our choice, you know." I tried to sound like my failure didn't haunt me, that the dreams I had last night never happened.

"I know. Colt has told me that a thousand times."

I didn't know what Sean was trying to say, if he was trying to say anything at all. I didn't feel comfortable giving him advice, and to be honest, I didn't have a lot of interest in giving him any. Colt could help him get through his issues. I would probably only set him back a few years if I tried.

"Want to head back?" he asked.

"Sure, it'll be lunch time by the time we get there."

I expected him to be not much of a conversationalist on the return hike, but he surprised me. He seemed to be more alive and in a better mood than just a few minutes earlier or the last few times I had noticed him. The lifeless look on his face disappeared. We discussed the wildlife that lived in the mountains around us and the development that now encroached on portions of their natural habitat. That led into the prices of real estate in the area and the pros and cons of living at nearly seven thousand feet above sea level.

Just before we reached the lodge some clouds blew in from the northwest and a light, but steady rain began to fall.

CHAPTER 16

Back in the lodge, I returned to my room to change clothes. The rain hadn't soaked through but they were damp, and my fall had left the right knee of my jeans soiled on the outside and bloody on the inside. The abrasion on my knee wasn't serious and only needed some cleaning.

By the time I reached the dining room for lunch, I found what was left of the hunting group huddled together at the same table they had selected earlier. A couple of them looked up and saw me, but returned their gazes to each other without acknowledging my presence. I strolled over to their table.

"How are you all doing?" I asked.

They looked up at me. No one rushed into conversation.

"Mr. West," Geri finally broke the silence. It also sufficed for all the conversation they intended to waste on me. Pretty much in unison they all looked back down at their meals or each other and ignored me. A couple resumed their internal discussions.

Part of me would've loved to have grabbed a nearby chair and squeeze in, uninvited, among them. However, most of me simply wanted to eat in peace, so I walked off to another table, not too far away and sat down. A young, female server approached me.

"Soup of the day is tomato basil," she said as she placed a glass of water down in front of me.

For some reason, she looked a little out of place in the dining room, although her short blond hair, blue eyes, and natural smile seemed pleasant enough.

"Haven't seen you here the last couple of days."

"My dad asked me to come in and help today. Two of the employees called in sick."

"After all that has happened here, I'm surprised more haven't," I said.

"More have. The two I mean worked the dining room. That's why he needed me here."

"Your dad, Rick, the manager?"

"Yeah, you know him?"

"No, not really. He must be stressed out over all this."

"Things got a lot better this morning," she said.

"Oh?"

"Uh oh, here he comes. What can I get you, mister?"

"How about the soup, a grilled cheese and some iced tea."

"Okay," she said and spun on her heals and headed to the kitchen.

"Good morning," Rick said. "I hope our staff is performing satisfactorily today."

"She's doing great," I said. Like most parents, I had no doubt that Rick supervised his children's work performance more than he did the rest of the staff. "How about you, Rick? How are you doing today?"

He looked at me silently for a second. He probably

wondered why I knew his name.

"Okay," he said with the hint of a smile.

"My name's Jim, Jim West. Join me for a bite?" I asked.

"Maybe for a cup of coffee," he said and sat down.

"All this crazy stuff must be awful hard on everyone here."

"It is. I just hope the Sheriff gets it all resolved soon."

"Me, too."

"Did you know the woman who hung herself?" he asked.

"Only met her here." I figured that was what most people thought, that she had committed suicide. I couldn't help but wonder if her ghost stood there somewhere close to us screaming that she hadn't hung herself.

"She seemed a little strange," he said.

I didn't respond, so after a few seconds I guess he felt the need to explain.

"I guess I shouldn't speak like that of the dead. It's only the way she dressed and acted. Most adult women whom I've known don't do that."

"She did wear some strange outfits," I said. "How did she act strange to you?"

"Oh, I don't know." At first I didn't think he was going to explain, but he did. "When they first got here, I saw one of the men grab her ass. He really latched on, and she smiled and snuggled up to him. It only lasted a second and no one else was around."

"Who was it?"

"I don't know. To be honest, I never did pay any attention to him. I assumed at the time they were a couple. Later, I found out she was the single one and all the men in the group were married."

"That's right."

"And that wasn't all. On that first night at the bar, she was dressed in all brown. I happened to be at the other end of the bar, just about ready to go home. I guess I must have been staring at her. She noticed me and blew me a kiss. That startled me and she started laughing."

"What happened then?"

"Nothing. I went home. I'm a married man, Jim. I don't fool around with strange women, and I do mean strange."

I guess he didn't consider Bev strange. He finished his coffee and went back to work. I ordered a slice of pie.

"Yep, that's my dad," the young server admitted when she brought my pie.

"Seems like a nice enough guy."

I noticed the hunting group get up from their table and leave in mass.

"Looks like I'm your only customer. Have a seat."

"Oh, I can't do that."

"Can I ask you a question that you might think is none of my business?"

"Of course, but you may not get an answer," she said it in a way that made me think that strange men had asked her unwanted questions more than once before

"How are these killings going to affect the lodge?" I didn't expect her to know the answer, but I was fishing for something else.

"Oh, I thought you were going to ask me something personal. I know my dad had been really worried, but I think he feels better about everything today."

"Do the police have a suspect?"

"I wouldn't know that, but my Aunt had to go into the hospital last night. She had a gall bladder attack. She's been a pest."

That would've postponed any family decision to remove Rick, I thought.

"How about with the employees? You mentioned some of them have stopped coming in."

"I think they're nervous, and I know in Jeff's case, his parents told him he couldn't work here anymore."

"That's too bad."

"I think parents are always overly protective."

"Will so many leave that the lodge will be shorthanded?"

"It already is. That's why I came in today."

"Do you think any of the employees may have been involved in the killings?"

"Wouldn't that be something!" she said wide-eyed.

"So there are no rumors that one of the staff here was a jilted former lover or a serial killer?" I said in jest.

"No, and I would've heard. Jeff and Melodie would have told me."

"So I'm safe staying here?"

"Oh! I didn't think about that, but I think you're as safe here as anywhere else. You know people die out on the highway every day."

After passing on that bit of wisdom, she sauntered back to the kitchen, and I finished my pie. I hadn't thought that one of the employees was involved in either death, and while my opinion along with the gossip at the lodge might not be considered proof, I still had my money on one of the ever diminishing group of hunters.

My phone buzzed in my pocket.

"West? This is Detective Bruno."

"Are you calling me from upstairs?" I wondered why he just hadn't sent someone around to gather me.

"No, I'm at my office. I'd like you to come down here for a minute."

"Can't…" I started to ask him why he couldn't discuss whatever it was over the phone, but changed my mind. "Sure. I just had lunch, I can come right over. How do I get there?" A trip away from this lodge would do me good.

Bruno gave me directions, and ten minutes later I steered my Mustang away from the Royal Lodge.

Driving through a lot of New Mexico can be boring: flat and few trees. However, the rest of the state explains why they call New Mexico the Land of Enchantment. Winding down this portion of the state highway, I wished someone else was driving, so I could better enjoy the scenery. For a while I forgot about the dead and dying in the world and wondered how the early settlers must have felt traveling through this part of the country.

Sections of the highway still held on to some of the rain that had fallen earlier, which required my paying attention to my driving.   The first large puddle I hit nearly sent me hydroplaning off into the trees. Fortunately, the puddles were few, and now that I watched for them, they were easily seen early enough to take defensive action.

A bobcat scurried off the road ahead of me as I approached the town. I slowed and tried to see where it went as I passed by, but it had blended too well into the underbrush. As my five year old neighbor would say, "Awesome!"

I found the sheriff's office on my first try. An older building that lacked appeal. Despite the invite I had to wait in the outer lobby area for nearly twenty minutes. During that time no one else came in or left. Slow business for law enforcement is good business. What was the old saying? Hours of boredom interrupted by moments of sheer terror. Something like that, and just as applicable to firemen, I thought.

The deputy who came to get me reminded me of a newly minted lieutenant in the military. His uniform looked crisp, clean, and pressed to perfection. I doubted if he took a step out of this building during his work day.

"Mr. West?"

"That's me."

"Please follow me. Detective Bruno is waiting for you."

I felt like correcting him and telling him that I had been the one waiting. He may have been an inch or two over my six feet, but I had him by a few, well maybe more than a few pounds. I knew I would never see that weight again, unless someone dropped me off on a desert island and left me there for a few months.

After following him around three or four corners and up a flight of steps, I started to wonder how long it took employees to find their way around. The building seemed larger than it had looked from the outside.

"Here he is, Detective," the young deputy announced

suddenly when we came to an open door.

"Come on in, Jim." He stayed seated behind his desk and motioned me with his hand to have a seat across from him. "Thanks, Brent. I'll call you when Mr. West here needs to be escorted out."

I looked back at the door, but young Brent had already disappeared.

"You getting them right out of junior high now?" I asked.

"Seems like it, doesn't it? They look younger and younger every year."

"Yeah, and someone needs to feed that guy."

"Ha! Were you ever that thin?"

"Maybe back in high school and college."

"I don't think I ever was," said the detective with a big grin. "Some of these young guys and girls order salads at McDonalds." He shook his head, "What's the world coming to?"

"Who knows? Before long the government will likely ban red meat and grease."

"Don't say that. I'd have to hang up my badge at that point. But Jim, more to the point, we found the screen."

"Oh, you did. Good."

"We found it tossed in some bushes in the woods not too far behind the lodge."

"Any prints?"

"No, and that's the important piece. There should have been some, even if they were smudges, but the screen frame had been wiped clean before being tossed."

"How about that." I said as a statement rather than a

question. "That does imply that the window might have been open when the shot was fired and then closed before anyone noticed."

"May also explain why the killer took out Randi."

"If she was the accomplice who had closed the window after Benson had been shot and before screaming for help."

"We had already found partials of her fingerprints on the window," he said.

"Oh, way ahead of me," I said.

"Well, you started us down this path."

"Anything new on Randi's death?"

"Only confirmation that she was murdered."

I raised my eyebrows.

"Someone strangled her first with the same rope that was then used to hang her. Probably thought he was being pretty smart, but two sets of ligature marks will give it away every time. And both are distinctive. We have no doubt. The murderer almost messed up though."

"What do you mean?"

"She wasn't yet dead when he strung her up, just unconscious. Wouldn't have been a problem if you hadn't come along. She would've slowly suffocated."

"Yet she did die."

"Yes. She was too far gone when you got to her. But, a couple of minutes earlier might have been enough."

I didn't know if I wanted to respond. I didn't think he intended to blame me with getting there too slowly, yet it almost sounded like it.

"All I'm saying is that the killer should have made sure she was dead before he hung her."

"It has to be the same person that shot Benson. We can't have two murderers plus an accomplice out there, can we?" I asked.

"Hell, they could all be in it together. Maybe they got rid of Randi 'cause she was falling apart."

I let this sink in for a minute, and he let me. "Possible, and might make an intriguing theory, but I don't believe they're all in it together."

"I don't know," he said. "Can't see why it has to be just one of them."

"But you think like I do, that the murderer, or murderers, is someone within the hunting group?"

"I can't see any other solution. I could've been persuaded before the second murder, but not now. I still don't see the two Bettes being involved. There's no evidence that either of them have ever had any contact with the group before, and their alibi for the Benson's murder is solid."

I've seen many a solid alibi go down the drain before, but I tended to agree with him that the Bettes were innocent.

I nodded. "Discover any remote connections that the staff might have had with them?"

"Nope," he said.

"I've talked to a couple of the employees, too, and I can't see them involved either."

"Which takes us back to our original suspects, and other than a couple parking tickets, they all appear squeaky clean."

"Have any of them admitted leaving the shooting range, or been identified by the others as leaving the range for a few minutes about the same time someone shot Cross?"

"All of them went in and out of that building that housed the range. One to make a call, one to receive one, one to look for a different rifle sight, and so on. It's almost like they are clouding the whole thing on purpose."

I thought about what he said for a few seconds. Unless Cross had done something very bad to all of them, I couldn't believe they were all in this together.

"Have you determined the value of the company?" I asked.

"A lot based on my standards, and people have been killed for a lot less. Mrs. Schutte would receive the most on paper, but as a minority owner of the company she's done well. The disruption to the business, if not the total breakup would be bad for them all, including her. I mean if you're making a hundred dollars a week and have the potential to do that for a year or two, why throw that away for a quick thousand?"

"I get your point. Plus, I can't see Geri lifting her up and maneuvering that rope around her neck."

"I can't either," he said.

"So what's the plan?" I asked, not really expecting an answer.

"They're going to leave tomorrow. A couple of them have already talked to a lawyer, someone's brother. They know we can't keep them much longer. We're doing another round of interviews here this time. Maybe we can shake something out. That's why I wanted you to come to the station, too. I'd like them to think we also put you through the ringer."

"I take it that you'd like me to see what they might be saying when they get back to the lodge."

He nodded.

"They've already locked me out. They aren't talking to me."

"Really?"

"Yeah. No doubt one, two, or more of them know for sure that I'm not the killer, but they've created an atmosphere among the group that I'm the likely suspect. That or they already suspect me talking to you about them."

"Damn. Well, still, do what you can. We need to wrap this up in the next day or two or it'll become very difficult."

I knew that everyone's departure out of not only the local jurisdiction, but out of state, would severely hamper the authorities' ability to resolve the two murders.

"Is there anyone in the hunting group that you believe you can eliminate as a suspect?"

"No," he said shaking his head. "They all have given each other an alibi for the first killing and none of them admit to knowing anything that can help us on the second."

"How about, Geri, Mrs Schutte? Were you able to verify that she might have taken the medication?"

"No, but even if we did, we wouldn't know if she took it before or after Randi's death."

"That's true. Guess you can't arrest them all and see what shakes out."

"Not unless I'd like to change careers shortly thereafter."

"I know," I said. "Look, I'll do what I can, but I'm just a civilian now. I'm retired and I don't know these people. I don't think they like me or trust me, so don't get your hopes up."

He grinned, "Aren't you curious?"

"Sure I am. I'm also a bit irritated because I had started to like Randi, and I thought Benson was a nice enough guy."

"I've heard some interesting things about you, Jim."

"Don't believe everything you hear."

"I don't, but I'll be honest with you. We need some help with this one, and I'm not too proud to ask for it."

I didn't know who he had talked to or what he had read in a file somewhere, but I imagined if he looked hard enough he would find more than a few people in law enforcement who considered me a nuisance or worse. Since my retirement from the Air Force, fate had sent me down a journey I would never have chosen for myself.

We talked for a few more minutes before young Brent walked me back through the maze to the exit.

CHAPTER 17

A Starbucks sat on a corner next to a gas station and a hardware store not far from the Sheriff's offices. My presence doubled the customer total, and I had no trouble finding a table I liked.

I hadn't planned on having a one person pity party; I just knew I was agitated. What in the world had happened to me in the past five years? I had been happily married and a content career officer and special agent with the Air Force Office of Special Investigations. The divorce had come out of the blue, and my world had spun out of control.

My goal of living a peaceful life post-divorce and getting things back in order hadn't happened. My initial hope that my ex would come to her senses and want me back had dwindled away to a mere fantasy. Worse yet, since my departure from what had been reality to me pre-divorce, I had found myself in a hostile world where way too often I'd been forced to confront evil and danger. It's not that I didn't have to face similar threats in the service, but back then I was in control with a lot of resources behind me. I felt like someone else pulled my strings now and I had completely lost control.

I knew what had started my introspection. Detective Bruno's

remark that he had checked into me and implied he knew me. Since my so called retirement I had heard that before, too many times. What he had heard about me wasn't really me, at least not in my eyes, and I should know, right? He had heard about the Jim West whom fate had seized way too often lately. Once she had him, Fate had repeatedly tossed that Jim West into the arena where, like a gladiator, he had to fight his way out or die.

I wanted to be left alone. I felt like I had finally evolved to the point where I wanted a serious relationship with a woman. The last few years, my emotional baggage had ruined any potential with the few women I had met, and there weren't a whole lot of them in Clovis anyway. I had met a few, I thought, who held some potential, but they lived nowhere near Clovis. Maybe that explained why they still held potential.

A car shot down the road in front of the coffee shop and distracted me. A small, blue Mazda, but its driver, not the car, caught my eye. It looked like Bev from the lodge. The sight brought me back to the present. I wondered if she lived around here, where she might be going, and if she would be working later today at the lodge.

I finished my coffee and left Starbucks. I needed to toughen up a little. Bruno's remark shouldn't have bothered me so much, and I had to admit that I had allowed myself to become a little melodramatic. I hadn't been tossed into any so called arena on this trip. I could try to assist Bruno a little before I left, but despite my personal curiosity, this was his problem to solve, not mine.

I aimed my car toward the lodge, down the same road that Bev had taken a few minutes earlier. Clouds covered the sky and made the afternoon gloomy. It looked like we were in for more rain, but for the moment, whatever precipitation was out there held off. I knew snow had fallen lightly in this area about ten days ago, and while it might be nice to see, I didn't want to have to drive through it tomorrow when I returned home.

About half way back to the lodge, I drove up and over a small rise in the road. As I started down the other side, I saw that the road leveled off a few hundred yards in front of me, and, at that spot, the road seemed to turn from grey to black. It took me a brief second to remember the puddles I had driven through on my way into town. I took my foot off the gas and tapped my brakes.

I hit the puddle at what I thought would be a safe speed and was therefore surprised when the puddle still tried to take my steering away from me. With a little difficulty, I kept the car in my lane and reached the safety of the dry road. The puddle was actually a fast moving stream of water running across this low spot in the road. Somewhere up higher in the mountains the rain must have been heavy.

At the same time that I fought the steering, I noticed a blue car off to my right half hidden in the bushes. Once past the water in the road, I braked and pulled off onto the dirt and grass that made up the shoulder to the road. I left my flashers on and climbed out of my car to check out the blue car. It looked a lot like the one Bev had driven out of town.

Approaching it, I could see the tracks that the car had made in the soft, wet ground. They led right back to the point where the water ran across the road. Up close I could see that there didn't appear to be much damage to the car. What I didn't see was the driver. I looked around and didn't see anyone, but the thick forest blocked most of my vision away from the road.

I looked into the driver's side window but didn't see anything. I wondered if this was even the same car I had seen Bev drive, or for that matter, if Bev was actually the driver of that car.

A snap of a nearby twig caught my attention. I looked up and saw Bev walk into view.

"My hero," she said. "Have you come to rescue me?"

"Of course," I smiled. "Are you okay?"

"Nothing hurt but my car. It's stuck, and I think the right front wheel may be bent."

"Want me to try to rock it while you try to back it out?"

"No, I've already called Simon."

"Simon?"

"He works at a towing service. He also has the apartment down from mine."

"Okay, I'll wait here with you until he arrives."

"I have a better idea," she said.

"What's that?"

"I'll leave my car here for Simon, and you can give me a ride to the lodge. That's where you're going, right?"

"Yeah, but won't you need to be here?"

"No, he already told me if I got a ride before he showed up just to leave the keys under the passenger floor mat."

"Well then, let's go."

"Love the car," she said as she climbed in. "Put the top down, please."

"Might rain."

"Then we'll put it back up."

I couldn't argue with her logic. "It'll be a bit nippy."

"Good."

I turned the heater on full blast to try to compensate for the cool air that blew in on us. It helped, and I had to admit the car is always much more fun with the top down. I looked over at Bev. She had tilted the seat back further and was stretched out, eyes close, breathing in the fresh air. Her left leg stretched out straight and her right leg bent at the knee. Her conservative, nearly knee length, black dress rode up dangerously high. I willed my focus back to the road ahead of us. It wasn't easy.

"What time are you supposed to be at work?" I asked.

One eye opened and peered at me. "When I get there - no hurry. Hmm... this is nice. On a warm sunny day, you'll have to take me on a long drive." She closed her eye again, but suddenly opened both. "I almost forgot. I can't believe it. How are you feeling?"

"I'm okay."

"You found her last night. That must have been awful."

"It was."

Bev reached over and rested her hand on my arm.

I smiled at her, and did my best to keep my eyes on her eyes and not her legs.

"Did you hear that your friend Rick might be off the hot seat?" I asked.

"Yes, he called me this morning, all elated. He said that with all the attention she'll get with her gall bladder operation, that she'll soak it for weeks. Apparently, she loves being the center of attention."

I imagined the she whom Bev referred to was the sister that had given Rick such grief over his running of the lodge. The same one Rick's daughter had alluded to earlier.

"Now, if the sheriff can just catch the person that killed Cross and Randi, all will be well with the world."

"I thought that woman hung herself," Bev said. She stared at me waiting for a response.

I reached over and grabbed her hand in mine. "Listen, I don't know how quiet the police intend to keep this, so let's make this our little secret."

"But I thought you found her hanging from the ceiling."

"Yes, but it looks like someone strangled her first and then strung her up."

"Oh my God, that's awful," she said. She pulled herself up into a sitting position. "This is scary. We have a homicidal maniac at the lodge."

"It's not good, that's for sure, but I don't think he's picking random victims. I don't think either of us have anything to fear."

She looked at me. I figured she wanted to ask me if I was crazy. Two people murdered in two days in a small lodge, and I'm saying we had nothing to fear.

"I don't think the murders were random," I repeated, "and my guess is that there won't be anymore."

"Will everyone be leaving?"

"By tomorrow this time," I said.

"Is he going to get away with this?"

"I hope not."

"Me, too."

"I bet Rick would like for everyone to leave today."

"I'm sure he would. Can't blame him, and I would guess that most of the guests would like to leave today, too."

"Are you still leaving tomorrow?"

"Yes."

The conversation ended and we drove the remaining five minutes in silence. It dawned on me as we drove into the lodge's parking lot that despite my comments to Detective Bruno that I would try to learn all I could, I had done all the talking with Bev. I had given away information and learned nothing. Maybe my investigative techniques weren't that great after all, or maybe it was just those legs.

"I don't think the drinks are going to be free today, Jim, but if you join me in the bar later, I'll buy you one. I owe you that for the lift. Love your car."

"That's a deal," I said while I held the door to the lodge open for her. She went toward the bar, and I went to my room.

A note had been slid under the door to my room. "Due to the unpleasant events of the last two days, Management is offering a free dinner for all guests tonight...." The note went on to describe the meal offered, the times the dinner would be available, and another paragraph about how sorry Management was.

"Should have comped us a night or two at the lodge," I said out loud to myself.

For the second or third time since my phone call with Stu, I considered jumping back into my Mustang and driving home. I even threw my suitcase on the bed to start putting my few clothes into it, but rather than start packing, I stared at it for a few seconds and put it back in the corner of the room. One more night, then I will leave.

Someone knocked on the door to the room.

"Can I buy you a cup of coffee, or a beer, or something? I'd like to talk to you, if you have the time." Colt Bettes stood on the other side of my doorway.

"Sure," I said. "What's up?"

"I'm not sure."

We walked down to the bar. I don't mind drinking coffee in the afternoon, or evening for that matter, but this trip had me more in a beer mood.

Bev raised an eyebrow at me when she brought us our beers but didn't say anything.

"What can I do for you?" I asked after we beat around the bush for a while.

"I understand Sean had a discussion with you somewhere out in the forest behind the lodge."

"Yes."

"I realize you may think I'm prying, but what was the discussion about?"

"It wasn't about anything. He found a dead elk and said it reminded him of himself. About it being half there and yet not half there. Something like that."

"He would say that, his being an empty shell, but that's not it."

"Suppose you give me a hint. I'm not sure what you're looking for."

"Did he say anything about how ashamed of himself he was?"

"No."

"Are you sure?" he asked.

"What are you getting at?"

"I'm just trying to figure something out."

"Why did you want to have this conversation with me?" I asked.

"He's acting strange, no scratch that, different. He's acting different today." He paused, but I waited for him to start talking again. "He went up to the room where that poor woman hung herself last night. The room is still sealed off, and there's a deputy there. Sean went right up to the doorway to the room and stood there staring in. I guess the deputy got a little jumpy with him standing there and asked him to leave."

"Why did he go up there?"

"That's the interesting part. When the deputy asked him to leave, he said he wanted to stay, that he wanted to know how he would've done it."

"What?"

"I know. The deputy called his boss and a few minutes later two other deputies arrived and took Sean to one of the empty rooms."

"What did he tell them?"

"I don't know exactly, but about twenty minutes later I get a call in my room to come down to the lobby to take Sean off their hands, just like he was a child." He shook his head in slight disgust as he finished his sentence. "You know, simply because a person has emotional or adjustment issues doesn't mean he can't be totally functional. Hell, Sean lives by himself and takes care of himself."

"That's not why you wanted to talk to me, right?"

"No, of course not. It has to do with what you said to him."

"What was it that I supposedly said to him?"

For the first time since we sat down he grinned.

"Okay, sorry, I'm not being very clear. You know he came to your aid last night."

"He told me--"

"Ahh," Colt interrupted, "tell me about that conversation, and please don't leave anything out."

He was beginning to get under my skin, doctor or not.

"As I can recall, we didn't have much of a conversation about it. He said that he got to the room and I was already performing CPR. He said he didn't know what to do so he ran and got additional help."

"Yeah, I know all that, but that's not what I need. What did he say about you and the dead woman?"

"He said I appeared to be determined to keep her alive, which I was."

"But he didn't get involved?"

"He went for help. That was important."

"Yes, I know. Something in your conversation with him has hit a nerve with him."

"Not a bad one, I hope."

"No, no, a good one, I think. I'm trying to understand what you said that I haven't said a dozen times before. Somewhere, I must have missed something."

"Now you've got me confused. I promise you I didn't try to do any counseling on Sean. He was deep in thought when I found him out there standing on that ledge."

"Standing on a ledge?"

"Yes. I thought he was considering suicide."

"He does now and then."

"Well, this time he said he wasn't. The elk had him fixated."

"I don't want to discuss the elk. Think, man, think, what else did you say?"

"Look, Colt, I know you mean well, but I need to head out and check something on my car, so I'll talk to you later. Thanks for the beer."

He looked at me bewildered. "Wait, wait, I don't mean to be pushy--"

"But you are. Let me think over the discussion I had with Sean, maybe something new will come to mind. If it does, I'll be sure to let you know what it was."

I left him sitting there. If he wanted to browbeat someone, he could do that to his patient. Besides, Sean could tell about the conversation as well as I could, and definitely had the upper hand in knowing what had been significant to him.

A sheriff's cruiser pulled into the parking lot and four members of the hunting group piled out. The cruiser sped off and the four walked abreast toward the lodge. I met them on the steps. Well, meeting them might be understating what actually happened.

I realized when they were only a few paces away that they were not going to make any room for me to get through them. They had a tougher time than I had at the sheriff's office and were then driven unceremoniously back to the lodge in a cramped sedan. I empathized with them, but I hated to have to skirt to the far side of the steps.

There's a time to face down a bully or even a crowd of bullies, but this wasn't one of them. I move to my right.

"Guys," I said with a half-smile and a nod.

I'm not sure if I didn't move fast enough, or if Nesbitt moved toward me a little as we past, but his left side clipped me and knocked me into the far rail. If it wasn't for the rail I'd have sprawled out onto the ground. Instinctively, my foot shot out at his knee and ignominiously caught nothing but air.

No one noticed my futile attempt at exacting revenge, so at least I avoided further embarrassment. I straightened back up and watched them enter the lodge. Good thing I don't carry a gun, I thought. Popping off a few knee caps would have given me a brief high, but the temporary satisfaction would have resulted in longer term unwanted consequences.

I think at any age people can be quite dangerous in groups. It's not just dogs that can develop a pack mentality, and it can appear quickly. Alone against the four of them, I couldn't have done much anyway except satiate my pride by risking real injury to myself, and I knew pride could cause a lot of unnecessary trouble.

I walked out to my car and leaned against it. I breathed in the fresh mountain air and gave my blood pressure time to come back down. The air felt cooler now as the sun started to dip behind the mountains, and I sensed we had a good chance of rain coming in. A car pulled up. New guests, I wondered? However, when the two people in the car climbed out, I saw it was Vic and Geri. They didn't appear to be in good moods.

"I'm leaving tonight! You can stay here or come with me. I don't really give a damn!" Vic snarled and marched off.

"I don't know why you can't wait until tomorrow!" Geri yelled at her husband's back.

He ignored her, disappearing inside the lodge. She leaned over the top of the car, her head in her hands. I thought she might be crying.

Only a few yards separated us. "Are you okay?" I asked.

"Oh! You startled me, I didn't see you there."

I didn't see any tears in her eyes. "Sorry, I just wanted to make sure you were okay."

"I'm okay. I just have a headache."

"May I walk you inside? I asked.

"No."

I took that as a dismissal and started to walk away.

CHAPTER 18

"No, wait a minute. I didn't mean that the way it sounded. I don't want to go in right now," she paused for a few seconds, "but I would like some company. Would you mind walking with me to the firing range and back? I need to think some things out, and I'd rather not be wandering out here alone."

"I'd be happy to," I said, and I meant it. I didn't know if it was my own need to avoid the lodge and the four bullies for a while longer or the opportunity to walk and talk with Geri.

"Thanks," she said and started walking.

"Are you more concerned about running into the murderer out here or the lions, tigers, and bears?" I asked trying to soften the mood.

She grinned, "Actually none of the above. I need someone I can talk to."

My turn to grin. I wondered how much Colt Bettes charged per hour. If people kept wanting to talk to me, maybe I should consider going professional.

"I don't mind being a listener, but I'm not sure if I can be much help to you."

"That's okay. I don't even know if I'm looking for advice, or if I just need a sounding board. And Jim, that's your name right? Not James."

"Always been a Jim, never been a James."

"Well Jim, you're the perfect choice for me right now. We hardly know each other and by tomorrow this time we'll never see each other again."

"So I take it that your real motive is not to ask me to sneak away to Paris with you?"

"I've got so many issues right now, Jim, believe me you wouldn't want me."

I thought about arguing but didn't.

"I'm sure the two deaths have been devastating to you all," I said.

"It's like a bad dream. Both are horrendous by themselves. Together it's almost unbelievable. My whole world is falling apart."

"Will you have to dissolve the company?"

"I didn't think so at first, but now there's no way to rescue it. None of us trust each other, the police are breathing down our necks, there's going to be the mother of all audits starting next week, and I just want to crawl in a hole and hide. I also think I want out of my marriage."

We walked in silence for a few minutes. I didn't think she really wanted me to throw my two cents worth of advice into the conversation.

"Vic is demanding we leave tonight. The rest of us have already agreed to leave as planned tomorrow morning. He's leaving regardless what I decide."

"So is that why he got the rental?"

"Yes. I understand where he's coming from; someone has been dying here every day."

"Then why don't you leave?"

"Because when he gave me the ultimatum, I realized I didn't want to go with him. I don't want to go with him anywhere anymore. I've been fooling myself the last couple of years. I don't love him anymore."

"Well, then that's your answer."

"That's only one of my answers. But I have to admit, thinking that I'm going to leave him that I've actually made that decision, does make me feel a little better. You know, I really don't imagine he'll care. I think he's been seeing someone else lately anyway."

She remained quiet for about a minute before speaking again. "I know he'll try to soak me in the divorce."

"What does he do for a living?"

"He thinks he's going to be a great author."

"Has he written anything?"

"Not really, he's been fooling around with a couple of ideas for at least two years, but he's never shared a manuscript with me. I don't think he has one."

"Will he be able to go after the money you have sunk in the business?"

"I don't know, but I'm sure he'll try. I don't even know what the company will be worth now."

"How about insurance?"

"Oh yes, we had insurance on both Cross and myself. The insurance is supposed to help in the smooth transition of the company, but now I don't know."

We reached the firing range and made a big arc turning around.

"I guess when we get back I'll have to sit down with Mr. Hardzog. He may have some ideas. I just don't know."

"Even if everyone goes their own way, you and Hardzog still own the business. The cash flow that's already coming in will continue to do so, right?"

"For a while, but except for the older clients, most of the new ones were brought in by the guys. Those clients might go to wherever those guys land a new job."

"Won't any of the men stay with you?"

"I don't know. Harv might. He's the most level headed of the bunch. Maybe when things cool down they all will," she said. She didn't sound like she believed a word of it.

"Could one of them be the killer?" I asked.

"No. No way. Besides, didn't Randi write a confession on the wall before she hung herself?"

"What did they tell you in your interview today?"

"Tell me? Ha! They didn't tell me anything. They wanted to know if I drugged myself, and if so, when I did it. I told them for the millionth time that I didn't drug myself. I don't know how I got drugged, when I got drugged, or by whom I got drugged. I don't even know for sure if I got drugged, although I have to admit I had a very hard time waking up."

I believed her. There was no reason not to, and I had already dismissed her in my mind from being involved in Randi's death.

"You know," I said. "Randi didn't commit suicide."

"What?" She stopped walking and looked straight into my

eyes. "You aren't kidding me, are you?"   A sudden fear appeared in her face.

"No, not me." I held my palms up in a gesture of peace. "I happen to know a few things, but not because I killed anyone."

The fear faded. "What do you know?"

"Only some things that pretty well prove she was murdered, but I think Detective Bruno would like to keep that secret for the moment." He hadn't told me to keep it secret, although he might prefer I not tell anyone. However, if he wanted my help, I would do it my way.

"Are you a cop?"

"No. Did anyone have a reason to kill either Cross or Randi?"

"No, that's just it, I can understand how the suspicion might be on one of us, but for the life of me, I can't imagine a motive anyone might have."

"Any problems in the office with Randi?"

"Randi was different, but she worked hard and got along with everyone. Too good with some."

I waited for a moment to let her continue, but she didn't.

"Want to talk about it?"

"I thought Vic might have been having an affair with Randi."

"Did you say anything about it?"

"No."

We walked in silence for a minute. A hawk dove down low in front of us, and a squirrel shot into a hole in an old tree.

"People have been too quick to say evil things about Randi. The guys in the office were cruel in their comments about her.

She did have an affair with Aaron about six years ago. It lasted for a couple of months. When it ended, he started telling the guys things about her, you know, intimate things."

"Sounds like an ass."

"Sometimes, no, most times. The guys like him and he works hard, but he's not a good person. I talked to Cross about it at the time. I thought we should've fired him. It surprised me that Randi hung around after that. I would have quit immediately, but she hung in there."

"Tough kid."

"Yeah, I guess you could say that. Since their breakup, rumors would fly every time one of the guys went on a business trip with her or simply drove her home from the office. As far as I know, she had a couple of male friends outside the office she spent time with, but no one in the office despite the gossip."

"Then why do you think she and your husband might have been an item?"

"Just stuff," she said and left it like that. "How about you, Jim? Ever been married?"

"Once."

"Divorced?" She looked at me, and I nodded. "Married long?"

"Twenty years."

"Wish you were still married?"

"Yes," I said too quickly. Time to steer the conversation in another direction, but Geri did it for me.

"That's my problem. I didn't get married until late. I was in my mid-thirties."

"That seems normal now-a-days."

"It may be, but it's the reason I haven't left Vic earlier. I waited a long time to find who I thought was Mr. Right, only to find out later I wasn't a very good judge of men. If I leave him now, I'm sure I'll never find another man who would want me. My hair is turning grey, and as my friends say, our perky days are behind us."

"You're being too hard on yourself. There are a lot of single men our age wandering this earth."

"Men, our age as you put it, have a particular attraction to younger women."

I didn't necessarily agree with her, but I waited too long to give her a good argument.

"Could Nesbitt have killed Cross and Randi?"

She stopped walking. "Aaron? No. He looked at Cross as his mentor. He sucked up to Cross, and Cross knew how to stroke him. I think Aaron believed he would be Cross' chosen one when the day ever came that Cross retired. His death blows Aaron's dreams apart. He sincerely took Cross' death hard."

"Could he have killed Randi?"

"I don't know why you're so interested in this--"

"Aren't you?"

"Of course--"

"Well?"

"I just don't like gossiping. Okay, well, I think Aaron liked having Randi around because he felt superior around her. She was a living, wild game trophy he could brag about. If he killed her, he would be getting rid of his grand prize."

"Who's your first pick then?"

"You mean as the killer?"

I nodded.

"Like I told you, I can't see any of them doing it," she said.

"Well, if we eliminate you and me, the lodge staff and the two Bettes, we only have five choices."

"These Bettes guys, why is everyone discounting them?"

"They have a solid alibi for the time when Cross was shot." I knew alibis, even solid ones, fell apart now and then, but I wanted to focus on her group for as long as I could keep her talking.

"We have an alibi, too."

"It's a group alibi, the best and worst kind. It's like saying you were at a large party with dozens of witnesses. Easy to verify, but cops know it's easy to sneak away for five minutes and return, and no one would take any notice of it."

"Yeah, they asked me that over and over. People were going back and forth to the van to get things, and a couple of the guys received calls and went outside to talk. No one was gone for over a few minutes."

I stopped and pointed to the window I was now convinced someone had shot through to kill Cross Benson.

"This is where the killer took his shot. He could have moved in a little closer."

Geri stood still staring at the window. "Aren't you forgetting the window itself?"

"Not if it had been opened and then closed by Randi before she started screaming."

Her face paled, "Oh my God."

"It only took us a couple of minutes to get here from the

firing range. If the shooter brought the van, he would have been here in seconds."

"Randi kept saying how sorry she was last night. I had no idea that she meant she had anything to do with the Cross' death. She liked Cross. He was always kind to her."

"Maybe she never forgave him for not putting a stop to Aaron's remarks." It could be a possible explanation, I thought.

"But you don't think she pulled the trigger?" she asked still staring at the window.

"No."

Geri shivered. It had gotten colder out as the sunlight began to fade, but I felt like the cold hadn't caused the shiver.

"What is it?" I asked.

"Nothing, I want to return to my room now."

"Okay." We walked the rest of the way without saying anything.

"Thanks for inviting me to walk with you," I said as we entered the lodge.

Geri either didn't hear me or chose to ignore me. I stood in the lobby while she walked away.

"That's what happens when you expect a little squeeze and a smooch before the lady is ready for it." Bev stood there smiling a few paces away.

"I'm innocent," I said.

"I believe it," she said. "That's your problem."

"I'm not that innocent," I said.

"Believe me, you are."

I didn't know where the conversation was going, but I didn't need it. "Been busy this afternoon?"

"Only those two and they've been hitting the booze seriously." She pointed to Griffith and Stallings seated in the far corner.

"They don't look too happy."

"They aren't. They look like two angry dogs ready to bite the nearest mailman." She looked at me like the warning was meant for me.

"Don't worry, I won't mess with them."

"Can I buy you a beer?"

"Is everything still free?" I asked.

"No, I just wanted to know if I could buy you a beer."

"Sure," I said and moved to a seat at the bar. The door to the nearby office opened, and Rick came out holding the arm of a tall, slender woman. She wore khaki slacks and a red sweater. Her hair was an unashamed grey. They appeared very comfortable together as they moved to a table close by.

"Yes, that's Mrs. Rick," Bev whispered in a sour tone. "She rarely comes in here."

It sounded like Bev didn't like the competition, legitimate or not, coming into her space.

"Bev," Rick called to her.

Bev hustled over, took some drink orders, and went back to work behind the bar. I watched in amusement. She returned to Rick's table with a Scotch on the rocks and an Old Fashioned.

"Hope you got those right," I said to her in jest when she returned. She gave me a 'stuff it' look and walked down to the end of the bar to ask the two men if they were doing all right.

"Hey, Bev," Rick called again and Bev went over to his table. She came back carrying the Old Fashion. I suddenly wished I hadn't said anything before. She looked at me, and I realized that I might be taking a big risk by saying anything more. She dumped the drink into the sink and poured a glass of chardonnay which she then took to Rick's wife.

"Witch," she mumbled softly to me when she returned. "There wasn't anything wrong with that drink."

"Does she suspect anything?"

"I hope not." She turned away from me and walked to a spot about ten feet away where she fiddled with a few bottles and glasses.

"Bev," I said. "I'm sorry. I had no right to ask."

"It's not you. I sometimes wonder whom I'm fooling."

"Let's talk about something else. Did the police interview you today about the incident last night?"

"No, not really, I mean one of the deputies asked me if I had heard anything or knew anything about the incident that I wanted to talk about. I said no, and that was it."

"I only ask because they seemed to have pulled in a lot of us for further questioning."

"I know. That's been the main point of conversation down there." She motioned with her head toward Griffith and Stallings.

"It's only natural for them to be a little hyper by now. Their whole lives have been affected by this."

"So has everyone else's," she said.

"I know, but more so with them. I imagine they're taking it personally by now."

"Do you think they're involved?"

"Could be."

"When I think too much about it, I get a little frightened."

"Me, too. That's normal."

"For some reason, you don't strike me as the frightened type."

"This drink tastes stale," Rick's wife had walked up behind me. She held the glass out for Bev to take. The two women's eyes met. She may not have known about her husband's infidelity, but she obviously sensed something because the animosity that surrounded her was palpable.

"I'm sorry," Bev said. Even I could tell she didn't mean it. "May I pour you something out of another bottle?"

"No, but I do mean to speak to my husband about this."

I looked back and saw that Rick had gone off to a corner and was talking on his phone.

"Witch," Bev whispered again when Rick's wife had gotten back to her table.

"I wonder what he sees in her?" I asked purely to support Bev.

"Who knows?"

"His daughter seemed nice."

"She's a doll. Did you meet her in the restaurant?"

"Yes." I felt like asking Bev if maybe the daughter had heard some gossip from the other, younger employees, and had said something to her mother. However, I decided the whole topic might be best to avoid.

"There they go," she said. I turned and saw Rick and his wife leave the lodge.

"Hey," shouted Stallings from the corner, "another round!" He held his empty glass up in the air.

"Coming right up," Bev shouted back with a smile.

I wouldn't have been as polite, but she knew how to treat rowdy customers.   Besides, I didn't like any of those guys anymore.

I watched Bev walk over to the two.   When she placed the drinks on the table, Stallings reached behind her. From my angle, I couldn't see where he placed his hand, but Bev's quick reaction in knocking it away and stepping back out of range gave me a pretty good idea. Her smile disappeared.

"Hey! Keep your hands to yourself or get out."

"Sorry, ma'am, must be the booze. Didn't mean anything by it," Stallings held both of his hands up in the air in mock surrender.

"You okay, Bev?" I asked. I had walked over to their table.

"Yes, let's go sit down somewhere." She grabbed my arm, but I didn't budge.

I glared at the two men.

"You know, Mark here thinks you might actually be the guy that killed Benson, but I tell him he's got it all wrong. I told him you're a cop or maybe a snitch. You look like a snitch," Griffith said.

"Please, Jim," Bev tugged at my arm.

"I wouldn't bet against Mark's opinion, little man, and if he's right you might want to think about who's next."

I let Bev pull me away.

"Now why did you say that?" she whispered to me as we went to the far end of the bar.

"I guess it was kind of childish," I smiled, "but it was either slug one of them or say something stupid. Stupid won out."

"Well, I'm glad you didn't start a fight."

"I kind of wish I did," I said.

"Maybe we both ought to jump into your car and drive away for good," she said.

I smiled at her. "Maybe we should." Of course we didn't, and I sometimes still regret that we didn't.

CHAPTER 19

I returned to my room. My cell phone buzzed, and it surprised me to see a Virginia area code.

"Hello," I said.

"Jim, it's me, Stu."

"Everything okay?"

"Yes. I wanted to call and apologize, and if you're available, I was thinking I could come out there this Thursday. We could have our vacation one week late."

"No can do, Stu. I'm still here at the lodge having the time of my life. Sorry you missed it."

He paused, and I figured he was trying to see if I was pulling his leg or not.

"Are you really still there at the lodge?"

"Yes. It's beautiful here and ever so peaceful. Haven't slept so well in years."

"Well that makes me feel better. I was starting to feel guilty."

"You can still feel guilty."

"Maybe in a few months," he said.

"Yeah, but next time you fly in to Clovis, and we'll drive up together."

"That's a deal, man. I'll call you in a few months."

I hung up and wondered if my phone could be programmed to ignore calls from certain numbers. I lay back on my bed and tried to picture how Stu would have handled all that had happened at the lodge if he had come out. On the positive side, we could've bunked Stu and Sean together, and Colt would've had even a bigger chance to excel.

Having disposed of Stu by putting him with the Bettes boys, I thought about Bev and her predicament. Women have been having affairs with married men forever, and vice versa, but I still felt sorry for the people that got hurt in those love triangles. I acknowledged that there could be a million variables that ultimately led to a woman being attracted to a married man, and I knew fixing fault could be complicated, but in this case I felt sorry for Bev.

Logic did not factor into my feelings. I liked her and felt she could do better. Colt Bettes would probably say she had low self-esteem or some other character flaw. I just wished she would move on to some guy who could give her a future, and no, I wasn't thinking of myself.

Maybe screwed up relationships and lives were the norm, and those couples that managed to stick together were the anomalies. Life had become so free and easy that people actually expected to be happy; working hard for anything anymore was definitely not commonplace.

This time my room phone rang and brought my mind back to the present. I wondered if I had been dozing.

"Jim, it's Colt. Can I buy you dinner?"

"I'm not really that hungry," I lied. I'm always hungry.

"I'm sorry if I got pushy earlier today. I mean it. The dinner is to make it up to you, and to give me a few minutes to explain what I have figured out."

Okay, he had me there. "You're talking about here in the dining room?"

"Yes, I'm down in the lobby now if you'd like to come down."

"Give me five minutes, and I'll be down."

I ran some water over my face and decided my clothes were good enough for another meal here at the lodge. I did grab a sweater in case I wanted to go outside after dinner and the weather turned colder.

I saw him when I started down the stairs. He looked like he had been drinking too much coffee, or maybe more like my four year old neighbor when he has to go to the bathroom but doesn't want to stop doing what he's doing.

"Jim," he almost shouted and came over to shake my hand like he hadn't seen me in a year, rather than just a few hours.

"Are you going to be able to eat?" I asked.

He looked at me not understanding my cynicism.

"Oh, I'm plenty hungry. Come on." He started toward the dining room. For a moment, I thought he was going to reach back to grab my hand to drag me along. I probably looked obvious by quickly putting my hands in the safety of my pockets, but I did follow him.

"I figured it out, Jim," he said once we sat down.

"The murders or Sean's behavior?"

"Oh no, not the murder," he sounded like solving the murder would be beneath him.

"Hello again," a soft, pleasant voice spoke to us.

"You're still here," I said to Rick's daughter. "Hope they plan on paying you overtime."

That got a smile. "Are you kidding me? I'm not even on the payroll. But, in fairness, my parents are pretty generous to me."

"Colt, meet Susan, or is it Susie?"

"Either way," she said and smiled at Colt.

"She's the prettiest employee in this place," I said.

"Jim, comments like those don't usually impress young women, especially when they come from men our age," he said like he was admonishing me, "but it is hard to argue with the facts."

"You two are silly. What can I get you to drink?"

"You like wine, Colt?"

"Is the sky blue?"

"Then let me suggest a Zinfandel from the Heritage Oaks Winery. Cross Benson recommended it to me the first night I was here. It was very good and I feel like having some again tonight."

"Sounds good," he said.

Susan brought out the two glasses and took our orders.

"To Cross," I said holding up my glass, "may his killer soon be behind bars."

"Did you know the guy very well?"

"Not well, but well enough to know he shouldn't have died the way he did."

"For sure. Do you think the police will catch the killer?"

"I hope so."

"This is good wine. I'll have to remember it."

What was left of the hunting group, sans the Schutte's, entered the dining room and went to their favorite table.

"Think it's one of them?"

"Seems likely," I said.

"Kind of scary."

"So, Colt, what's the good news?"

"Oh yeah. Did you two talk about your inability to save that poor woman?"

"You mean Randi?"

"Yes."

I thought back for a second. I didn't think I talked about it. It wasn't something I needed to dwell on, but then I remembered.

"You know, he did make some comment about my trying so hard, but that she still died."

"That's it!"

For a second, I thought he was going to high five me, or at least shout eureka.

"What do you mean?"

"Well, it's really complicated and not easy to explain in a few words." I translated that to mean that I might be too stupid to understand the explanation.

"You have a short, sixth grade version of the answer?"

"Ha! I didn't mean it like that, but I'll try. One of the demons that has kept him from moving on since the incident has been his failure to act in any manner to help that poor woman."

"The woman who showed up, almost dead, at his cabin years ago?"

"Yes. His inability to respond and provide her assistance has been an issue we never could get past. I reassured him as did others that there was very little he could have done for her, but our efforts never penetrated his guilt."

"I didn't say anything to him that might have helped, at least nothing I can think of."

"No, Jim, you don't understand." Maybe he couldn't help being condescending. "It's not what you said, it was the fact that you tried so hard and the woman still died. He saw you try. He knew you were going at it like a person obsessed with saving her. He said you wouldn't let anyone pull you away."

I listened with mixed emotions. He almost sounded that he was happy that the woman died, but I couldn't believe that he meant it that way. It reminded me of one of my boxing matches as a doolie, or freshman, at the Academy. We were in the middle of the third and final round. Up to that point it had been anyone's fight, suddenly my opponent hit me with a right that I never saw coming. My mouthpiece went flying and I saw stars, but I didn't go down. The ref rushed in between us and asked me if I was all right. For some inexplicable reason, my head nodded that I was, and the ref reached down and picked up my mouthpiece. He placed the mouthpiece, now covered with white powder from the canvas and a reddish hued drool that hung down from it, back in my mouth. The ref motioned for the fight to resume, and we stood there toe-to-toe and continuously clobbered each other for the last sixty seconds in the manner of true amateurs. I remembered I lost that match, but it was the only bout where afterwards all the upperclassmen from my squadron who were present came up to me, patted me on the back, and praised my efforts. The loss mattered, but my willingness to stand there and keep fighting won their admiration.

"Are you listening to me?" Colt asked.

"Oh, I was just remembering something."

"About your wife?"

"No," I wondered what made him think that.   "No, something else."

"Anyway, it's only one more brick in the wall, but every step forward helps."

"I would have thought that the shock of her appearance at his cabin and the subsequent experience with the police would have caused the majority of his problems."

"They may well be the biggest factors, but sometimes it's something specific, something behind the scenes, that the patient has to overcome first before they can face everything else."

"But you said that you had discussed his guilt before."

"Oh, sure, hundreds of times. But I obviously never really honed into it as I should have. His treatment by me and others has always been focused primarily on handling the shock of that poor woman showing up there and the subsequent psychological trauma he went through with the police. His guilt issues have been a side issue."

"And maybe it shouldn't have been?"

"Right. I mean who wouldn't feel a little guilty about not being able to help? Don't you feel bad about your inability in saving that woman?"

That woman. I didn't think of her as that woman. I didn't even like the way it sounded. Perhaps Randi had become closer to me in death.

"Of course I do," I said.

"Well, to the rest of us, his guilt was a normal reaction. We encouraged him to get past it, but never focused on it as a serious piece of the puzzle that had to be resolved before the rest of his puzzle could be put back together. Besides it's actually a subset of the guilt."

"The what?"

"That even if he tried his hardest back then to save her, she still would've probably died. We encouraged him to move pass his guilt because her death wasn't his fault. However, we never honed in on his lack of real skills to save her."

I wondered why not, but didn't ask. It had already gotten too complicated for me.

"So you think he might be on the road to recovery now?" I asked.

"I wouldn't go that far. That puzzle I referred to isn't a two dimensional one. There are layers to it, and there's nothing one can actually see to evaluate progress."

"So, do I get part of your fee?" I asked, trying to lighten the conversation.

"Like I said, this case doesn't pay."

"I know, just kidding you."

"He seems to like you, Jim."

"Maybe he just sees me as a kindred spirit."

"Could be. No offense, but it's easy to see you're carrying a lot of baggage."

"Are you always this flattering, or are you just looking for another patient?"

"No offense intended," he said and somehow kept a straight face.

"Can I get you a dessert?" Susan had come to my rescue. "We have a very good Boston Cream Pie."

"No," Colt said.

I would've have liked to have used the moment to make my escape, but the dessert won out.

"I'll have a slice."

"I'll find a big one for you," she said. She'll go far, I thought.

"Jim, I appreciate your talking to me. This is the most optimistic I've felt with Sean's condition in a long time. If you don't mind, I think I'll head back to my room."

"Not at all. If I don't see you before I leave in the morning, good luck."

We shook hands and he left.

Susan walked up to the table. "You're staying aren't you?"

I sat back down. "Of course, I'm not missing out on that dessert."

She placed the oversized slice of Boston Cream Pie on the table in front of me.

"I think I need a cup of coffee to go with that."

"Coming right up."

The dessert tasted great. The perfect attitude adjuster after the conversation with Colt. I looked up and saw Geri walk into the dining room alone. She started to head to the table where her colleagues were seated but spotted me and changed directions.

"Jim, mind if I join you for a second?"

"No, please do." She wore a flowered blouse and dark

slacks. A nice look, I thought. I could see her as a CEO.

"I want to apologize for this afternoon."

"Apologize?"

"Yes, for dragging you off with me and making you listen to my woes. I needed to vent. Sorry I picked on you to listen."

"Hey, not a problem. Walking through the woods with a pretty lady does wonders for my ego."

She smiled. "I think you're a nice guy, Jim. I wish we could have met long ago."

"Me, too."

She flashed a smile at me again and left to join her friends. I could feel that second smile. It kind of hung there and wrapped around you like a warm blanket on a cold night.

"Get a grip, man," I said to myself. "I must be the easiest pick up in the world." I took another bite of my dessert.

CHAPTER 20

I walked out of the dining room intending to head up to my room.

"Jim, hey Jim!" Bev called me from the bar.

I walked over. "What's up?"

"They dropped off my car a few minutes ago. I was tied up and couldn't leave." She nodded to a foursome I had not seen before.

"Are they staying here?"

"Yes, can you believe it? They hadn't heard about the excitement we've had. They're over there discussing whether to stay or leave."

"Get a few drinks in them and their courage will grow."

"Will you run outside with me in a minute to help me check my car?"

"Sure, but let me go up to my room for a second. I'll be right back."

"Okay, thanks."

I returned in a few minutes. I had put on my jacket in case we spent too long outside. Her car had been washed and looked fine.

"Not as much damage as you thought?" The two light poles

provided enough light to allow us to inspect the car.

"No. Had to get a new tire, realignment and balance, but nothing bent or broken. All in all, I say I was lucky. I let the water catch me by surprise."

"Well, it wasn't easy to see."

"True, but it flooded there last year, and I almost did the same thing. Think I would've learned."

"They cleaned it up. Looks nice."

"Thanks. It needed a good washing even before today, but that's an expensive way to get a car wash."

"Better than being rolled off a cliff," I said remembering an incident that happened last year.

She looked at me inquisitively but didn't say anything.

"Have you taken it for a test drive?" I asked.

"No. That'll have to wait until I get off, but they drove it here, so they should've noticed if anything was wrong."

"That's true, and I'm sure they would have been happy to fix anything else that needed repair. In fact, sounds like your friend runs an honest shop. Most places would've taken advantage of you and fixed a few things that didn't need it."

"Brrr, I'd better get back inside. Thanks for coming out here with me, Jim."

"No problem."

"I don't know why, but I didn't want to come out here alone. Sorry."

"Don't worry about it," I said as we walked back inside.

The foursome that had been debating whether to stay or not walked out of the lodge seconds after we returned.

"They leaving?" Bev asked the young man behind the

reception counter.

"Yep," he said shaking his head.

"Can't blame them," Bev whispered to me as we walked toward the bar.

"But it's too bad. The notoriety will probably hurt business for a while."

The front door of the lodge opened behind us and three people walked in. One had a big camera strapped around his neck. One of the others, the sole female, carried an iPad or one of its clones.

"Or maybe not," I said.

"What?"

"That may be the press."

We both watched from the bar as the trio checked into the lodge. The one with the camera began sweeping the interior with his camera. I turned around. I had no desire to get my face on local, or worse yet, national television.

A moment later, Bev realized what the cameraman was doing. "Oh, I think that man is videoing the lodge." She looked over at me. "That's why you turned around. You knew it didn't you?"

I nodded.

"Why didn't you warn me?"

"You look great. If it gets on TV, you should charge Rick for the business you bring in."

"I'm not sure if that was a compliment or not," she said.

I didn't have to explain myself because the trio grabbed a table next to the bar and asked for some drinks.

I took advantage of the mirror to watch Bev talk to them for a while before going to fetch their beverages. After she left, the one with the tablet typed in some notes. The other two reviewed something on the camera screen. I assumed they were looking at the video they had just taken of the inside of the lodge. More than likely they had also taken some of the outside, despite the darkness. They also spread four or five sheets of paper out on their table.

Bev returned to their table with their drinks: two glasses of red wine and a mixed drink of some sort. They talked to Bev some more and held up a sheet of paper for Bev to look at. She nodded at them about something before leaving. Rather than come directly back to me to talk she fiddled around cleaning a counter that already looked clean and moved a bottle or two from one shelf to another. Then, like it was an afterthought, she walked over to me.

"They are the press," she whispered to me. "They wanted to know what I knew about the two murders, except they weren't sure yet if the second was a suicide or a murder. I guess the Sheriff hasn't released a definitive answer yet."

I felt like asking her why she was whispering, but instead found myself whispering back at her. "What was on the sheet they showed you?"

"That was the most interesting part. They showed me an old press clipping about Sean Bettes and the poor young woman whom he was suspected of killing."

"I'm sure that they would love to find a connection with the recent deaths."

"I think they think that they already have, Sean Bettes."

"Yeah, I forget. They don't need the truth. They can create any link they want to and make the story as juicy as they can."

"Poor, Sean, and I don't even know the guy. They can really smear him again."

"Not good for his long overdue recovery."

I don't think she followed me. "Should we warn him that they are here?" she asked.

"It would probably be a nice thing to do, but they are watching us at the moment. Let's wait a while."

Vic walked into the bar. Rather than come to the counter, he took a table not far from the press contingent. He didn't pay them any attention, but they watched him closely.

Bev went out to see what he wanted to drink and ended up talking to him. I could tell she warned him about the press because his eyes went instantly to them. They talked some more before she returned and grabbed him a glass of wine. After she dropped off the wine, Bev returned to me.

"He's checked out and is leaving tonight. He said he'll find a place in Santa Fe for the night. Guess I can't blame him."

"Is his wife going with him?"

"I assume so." She looked at me like she was trying to read my mind. "Why are you interested?"

"I know she wanted to leave tomorrow with the rest of her group. I guess she sees it as a final show of cohesion before they go back to El Paso, and their group probably falls apart for good."

"He said he was fed up with everything going on."

"I wonder why he's hanging around then?"

"He's probably waiting for his wife, maybe she decided to go with him after all."

"Could be, but she was pretty adamant this afternoon."

"Think he could be the killer?"

"Definitely possible. He's on the short list, but that's a no brainer."

"Maybe for you," she said. "How about his wife?"

"Possible, but not likely."

"Not on your short list?"

"No."

"How about me?" she asked. Her eyes had a little twinkle in them.

"You're on my list, too."

She looked at me surprised.

"Just a different list," I said. This time it was my turn to smile.

She reached out and squeezed my hand.

"You know, I think I need to leave this place."

The sound of the female reporter striking up a conversation with Vic gave me an excuse to turn my head toward them and, at the same time, change the topic. The reporter held out a sheet of paper for Vic to review. Suddenly, Vic got agitated.

"I think that guy is here now! Did he do this?" He spoke loud enough for the whole room to hear him.

"She must have shown him the page about Sean Bettes," Bev whispered to me.

"I think you're right."

"If the police know this, why haven't they arrested him?" Vic asked the reporter.

The woman answered him in a softer voice. I couldn't catch what she said.

Unfortunately, Vic looked up at me and pointed the reporters in my direction.

"Talk to that guy. He knows more about this than the rest of us do, if he's not involved."

All three turned their heads toward me.

"I don't really know anything at all," I said.

"Would you mind answering a few questions for us?" The question came from one of the male reporters. The one with the red wine.

"How about tomorrow afternoon? I have a few things I need to take care of this evening."

"One o'clock tomorrow?"

"Sure."

"Right here?"

"Yeah," I said, "right here."

"You aren't going to be here tomorrow, are you?" Bev whispered again.

"No."

I looked over at Vic and the female reporter. She had taken a seat next to him, and he was talking up a storm with her.

"Wonder what he can be telling her?" Bev asked.

"Who knows?" But I was wondering, too. Nothing he said would do his wife's company any good. The notoriety of being implicated in a series of murders rarely does a business that needs customers any good. It could be particularly damaging if he started speculating why the murders occurred and who might have been involved. Of course, I knew that Vic might not be telling them anything about the murders. It was just as possible that he would take this opportunity to rant about the police harassing them.

"I don't like that guy," she said.

"I don't either." I didn't elaborate that I really didn't care for any of the guys in the hunting group. While Vic wasn't part of the foursome that ran me off the steps out front, I still considered him one of them and Geri's comments only reinforced my dislike.

Harv entered the bar, saw me, and walked over to me.

"Hey, I want to apologize for what happened out there today." He motioned with his head toward the front of the lodge. "I thought it was stupid at the time that we wouldn't budge, and I certainly didn't know that Aaron was going to knock you over."

"What?" Bev asked.

"Nothing," I said to Bev. Childishly, I felt embarrassed that she had learned what had happened to me.

In some male egotistic way, Harv must have sensed my feelings and didn't elaborate. "Anyway," he continued, "I'm sorry." He held out his right hand, and I shook it.

"No problem, man, I've been through a lot worst."

"Can I buy you another beer?" he asked.

"Oh, no thanks, I've had plenty. Besides, see that trio over there." I pointed to our visiting press contingent. "They're with the press, and I really don't want to talk to them."

"The press? I guess that makes sense. I don't want to talk to them either. Take care," Harv said and walked off.

"What was he referring to?"

"I had a small confrontation outside with the four of them earlier today. It was really nothing."

I don't know if I satisfied Bev's curiosity, but she didn't pursue the topic any further.

"This should get interesting," she said.

I looked behind me and saw Sean Bettes approaching me.

"Hey Jim," he said. He looked like he didn't have a care in the world.

"How're you doing?"

"Okay," he said. "Can I have a Coke?" his question directed at Bev.

"Of course."

"Sean," I said in a low voice, "that group right there is with the press. They have an old article about you."

"Oh," some of the color disappeared from his face.

"That's the guy you want to talk to!" Vic shouted from his table.

All three members of the press team turned and stared at Sean.

I felt he might take off in a run again, so I gently grabbed the back of his arm.

"Let's just leave," I said to him.

"Okay."

"Can we have a word?" The female arrived quickest. We had barely taken a step.

"Later," I said. "Tomorrow, like I told you, and only if you don't bother us ahead of time."

"How about you, Mr. Bettes?" her eyes stared right at Sean. "Are you going to let him do all the talking for you?"

"I have nothing to say."

We started walking off.

"Mr. Bettes! Are the two deaths here at the lodge related to the woman who died fifteen years ago? You know whom I'm talking about, don't you Bettes?"

Sean didn't respond. We walked out the front door of the lodge.

CHAPTER 21

The evening air seemed a little warmer than normal, even warmer than just a few hours earlier.

"I think it's going to rain," Sean said.

In the darkness I wondered how he knew. Of course, he may have just seen a weather report on the television.

"When are you leaving?" I asked.

"In the morning."

"Think you can evade the press until then?"

"I'll do my best."

Something large and dark flew overhead. I wondered if any owls lived up here.

"Actually, this has been a good trip for me," he said. "I know that may sound bad, and I do feel sorry for the two people who died. I only mean that for me it's been a good trip. I didn't anticipate for one second that it would be, but it has. The first day was very emotional. It brought back a lot of little things I had forgotten. Then to be here when another murder occurs, to be questioned again by the police, and later, when I found you and that poor woman. You were trying so hard to save her. It's like Colt had created some type of immersion therapy that he tossed me into."

I didn't know what I should say, so I remained silent.

"I know Colt has talked to you about me. I'm okay with that. I woke up this morning feeling more refreshed than I have in a long time.   That also must sound bizarre. I can't really explain it."

"No need to explain anything to me."

"Thanks. I hope Colt didn't indicate that I'm a total basket case, because you know, for years I've lived alone and have taken care of myself. For a while, just after the incident, I do think I was in some kind of shock. I didn't really understand it at the time. That's when I needed Colt the most, but none of us except maybe Sandra saw it. I only talked to Colt a few times back then. When Sandra left me, that's when the depression really sank in."

"My wife left me. I know how it feels."

"I tried a couple of times to end it all. I guess I didn't try too hard. Colt refers to them as gestures or calls for help. I guess they were. That's when he started working hard with me. Did he tell you that I lived on the streets for three years?"

"No."

"I guess it was my way to escape. One day, though, I realized that life would be more comfortable under a real roof. For the past seven years, I've been doing fine, although Colt may argue that point. I've worked a few different jobs and have paid my own way. I know there's a big difference between the old Sean and the current one, and Colt has seen that as something that can be fixed."

He stopped talking for a while.

"Has it been?" I finally asked.

"I don't know. I wanted to go on that hike this morning. Hard to explain, but I don't know the last time I wanted to simply go for a walk and explore the outdoors."

"Sounds positive," I said, having no real idea what it meant.

"Yeah."

"Can you drink coffee at night? I mean, will it keep you awake?"

"It doesn't bother me."

"Will you have a cup of coffee with me in the dining room? I won't force you to listen to any more of my stories, and I'd like to stay away from the press."

I wasn't in the mood for coffee or more conversation with Sean, but I heard myself agreeing to the coffee.

"Let me run back up to my room for thirty seconds, and then I'll meet you in the dining room," said Sean.

"Okay, I'll be in in a minute."

He left, and I stayed there leaning against the rail. The night was pleasant, and I wondered if the slightly warmer than expected air foretold the arrival of a front. Thick clouds moved slowly to the northeast, barely above the tree tops. Sean's prediction of rain seemed likely.

"I still don't know why you want to leave tonight!" Geri and Vic walked out onto the front porch.

"I told you, I'm sick and tired," he noticed me standing there and didn't finish his sentence. "Come on." He carried two suitcases, and Geri had a small carry-on.

"I'm not getting in that car."

They walked by me. Neither acknowledged my presence, and I decided not to interfere.

"You're not thinking straight, Geri. There's no reason to stay another night."

"We all agreed."

Vic responded, but they had moved far enough away that I only picked up pieces of their conversation. He tossed the two suitcases into the trunk of the car, took the carry-on from Geri, and placed it with the others in the trunk.

I started to walk into the lodge when their discussion took a nasty turn. Geri may have said something or maybe not, but suddenly Vic backhanded her hard across her face. She swung back at him, but he caught her arm and with his free arm, smacked her again.

"Hey!" I shouted, walking toward them. "That's enough. Break it up."

"You're getting in the car," Vic snarled at Geri.

"Screw you!"

"Let her go, Vic."

He looked at me. His eyes didn't look quite right.

"You couldn't stay out of this, could you?"

"Guess not. Now let her go."

"Maybe you both better get in the car."

I didn't know what he was getting at, but then I saw the gun. A nasty looking thing, bigger than it needed to be, a revolver, at least a .44 caliber, pointed directly at my stomach.

"You shoot that here, and you'll have the whole lodge out here in seconds."

"So what?"

So what? I wondered. What did he mean, so what? Did he really not care? The way he said it, it would have been a good bluff, but was it?   The sight of the revolver being pressed out ever closer to me brought me back to reality. It didn't matter if he meant it or not. I wasn't going to challenge him.

"Get in the car. You in the front passenger seat. Geri, you drive, now!"

"Vic."

"Shut up."

Geri moved around and got in the car. I climbed into the front passenger seat. Vic popped in behind me.

"Now drive. I'll tell you where."

Geri started the car and drove it out onto the paved road that led out to Highway 63.

"Go north on the road."

"Which way is that?" she asked.

"To your right, and don't speed."

"What's going on, Vic?" I asked.

"Just shut up and no one will get hurt," he said.

It didn't take a brain surgeon to realize he might not be telling the truth. "Hand me the purse," he said.

I felt like he addressed his remarks to me so I passed the purse to him.

"Now give me your cell phone."

"I left it in the room," I said.

"Don't lie to me. Give me your phone or start passing all your clothes back here to me."

I handed him my phone.

"Now everyone take it easy," he said.

Geri had apparently had enough of his bull.

"You killed them! Victor, you killed both of them didn't

you?!" she screamed.

"Keep us on the road," he roared from the back seat.

Geri steered the car back into our lane and somehow did manage to calm down a little. I didn't see another car on the road in either direction. Darkness dominated the landscape.

"You had already figured it out. I saw it in your eyes earlier today. That's why you had to come with me."

"No, Vic, I may have had my suspicions, but I didn't figure out anything. I certainly wouldn't have said anything to anyone."

"At some point, you would have."

"Why Vic? Why?"

"Just drive."

"But why would you want to hurt Cross?"

"Besides the fact that you slept with him, you mean?"

I looked at Geri. She looked surprised by his remark.

"Vic, if you know about that, then you know it happened years ago. Nothing has gone on between us since then. We both saw it as a mistake."

"And he wasn't the only one."

Geri looked more shook up by his comments than by the fact that he sat behind us with a big, fat revolver in his hands.

I wanted to say something, but I knew our presence in the car had little to do with Geri's past indiscretions. Vic had killed Cross and Randi. Nothing else made sense, but why? I thought playing dumb couldn't hurt my already bleak chances of getting away from him unhurt. Geri squashed that plan right away.

"Why? Why, Vic, did you do it?"

"Oh come on, Geri, certainly you can figure that out - the

money, of course. With Cross out of the way, a lot of money is shaken loose that comes to us if we dissolve the company."

"But we aren't going to dissolve the company. The money is there to take care of the company."

"That's just it sweetheart, you don't get a vote. That's why I needed you to come along with me on this ride."

The threat seemed to pass Geri by without her registering it. "You're talking nonsense. Did you kill Randi, too? Poor, harmless Randi - why would you hurt her?"

I wanted to turn and look Vic in the face. I also wanted to know why he killed her, but I needed him to think he had me too terrified to do anything.

"Randi was just a tool, a simple tool, a pawn to be used and discarded."

"I thought you…" Geri paused for a minute, and Vic answered for her.

"You thought I was having an affair with her? Ha! Sure I slept with her and even spent a buck or two on her, but that was just the plan. Talk about emotional baggage. She was loaded with it. She was as easy as a kid to manipulate. I told her we could get married, that I would take care of her, that we just needed the money to be free. She believed me, too. All she had to do was close the window after she discovered the body and then keep her mouth shut."

"But she didn't say anything! I spent a lot of time with her, and she never said anything."

"She would have."

"How could you?" Geri asked.

"You dumb bitch," Vic snarled. "You've always had money.

You've put everything into the company, and we have to live like everyone else, like common folk. Well, when I get the money, I'm spending it all on me, just me."

"We haven't suffered any."

"I've suffered just having to live with you. If I could've come up with a better plan, I would've killed the whole lot of you in an explosion."

I had no doubt he had looked into it.

"Do you plan to kill me, too?" she finally asked.

I felt like saying "Duh?" like my neighbors' teenage daughter has said to me a few times when I had made a not-so-witty remark.

"Of course, my dear, and your boyfriend here has given me so many ideas."

Geri took her foot off the gas. "Then you might as well shoot me now."

"Don't think I won't. I have nothing to lose. But how about if I shoot your boyfriend first."

I looked over at Geri. She looked at me. The car had slowed considerably. She looked at Vic and the way she looked right behind my head I sensed he had the weapon aimed at me. She pressed the accelerator down and we drove on. I felt the sweat on my body.

"Turn right just up here."

Geri took the lone turn off and we started driving on a narrow, thinly paved road. I looked to my right as we turned and saw the head lights of a car in the distance. Too far to be of any assistance but one could always hope.

"Take it slow, it won't be far from here. Yeah, having your boyfriend along gives me a lot of ideas. Maybe after I shoot you both, I'll tear up your clothing and scratch his face with your fingernails. Make it look like you killed each other after he tried to sexually assault you.   You know, boyfriend, if you want, maybe I'll let you take her, as long as you promise to be rough. Might be a nice way to go. What do you think?"

I didn't say anything, and he rapped the back of my head with the gun barrel. It got my attention but didn't seriously hurt me.

"I'm sorry," I said, keeping up my pretense of fear, "but I suffer from an old war injury and am pretty useless down there, if you know what I mean." I lied, but I didn't want him to pursue any of his crazy ideas.

"Then maybe I shouldn't call you boyfriend," he said. I felt like agreeing since I was already very tired of his saying it. "What do you think Geri? Guess you should just consider him one of your girlfriends now." He laughed at his dumb joke. Neither of us did.

"Slow down," he instructed.

I knew at some point I would have to make my move. He had already killed two people, and I had no doubt he intended on killing the two of us. However, I needed to get outside the car to have any chance at all. Luckily, the last thing Vic probably wanted was to leave any blood evidence in the rental car.

"I figure you're worth about two million to me dead," he said. "Does that sound about right?"

"I can't believe you think it'll be that easy," Geri said.

"You mean getting the money?"

"Yes. There'll be inquiries."

"Oh I have that covered, too. Here, stop here."

Geri stopped the car.

"Okay, now pull the car behind that row of bushes. Go this way." He pointed to the right. His hand was only inches from my head. Unfortunately, the revolver was not in it. The hand still tempted me, but the odds would be dismal, so I remained still.

Geri parked the car. I climbed out.

"Not so fast!"

I stood still beside the car. Geri took a lot longer to get out. Vic stood next to me, the car between Geri and us. I wanted to yell to Geri to run, but I waited too long, and the thought must not have entered her mind, because she hurried around the car to us.

"Vic."

"Shut up!"

He had backed up when Geri rounded the car. He probably thought as I did that she was going to get right in his face to argue some more, and he didn't want her that close. He turned on a flashlight and aimed it at Geri's face. She instinctively closed and covered her eyes. She also stopped walking.

"Now, you two, head up that path. Arm in arm, I don't want one of you straying. Oh, that's a cute picture, Geri. Just like you're out on a walk, with one of your girlfriends."

His girlfriend remarks annoyed me as much as his boyfriend one, but I felt better out here than in the car. Out here, one always had options. It didn't level the playing field, but my odds had improved. The night was very dark, the low clouds blocked whatever light the moon and the stars could have provided. Branches and leaves creaked, groaned, and rustled in the stiff breeze disguising the sounds of other movement around us.

Vic's beam of light lit up about ten feet of the path in front of us. We were in a thick section of the forest, and if I attempted an escape, I felt confident that all I needed was about twenty yards of separation and I could lose him. The trick was getting Geri to move with me.

"Hey you, what's your name again?"

I knew he was talking to me, but I ignored him.

"Hey!" he shouted.

"His name is Jim. Please don't shout, Vic," Geri's voice cracked as she talked. I looked over at her and saw tears running down her face.

Vic either didn't notice or didn't care.

"Jim, I can't tell you how happy I am that you decided to come along. This will make things so much easier."

"I aim to please," I said sarcastically.

"Yeah, I had lots of ideas to explain why Geri would be out here alone, but none of them sounded very good. Now, it's going to be a lot easier. She either came out here voluntarily with you or you forced her out here. Either way, you have to admit it makes more sense than her coming out here alone."

He had me there. I had given him a better story. Too bad for him I didn't plan on sticking around.

"You simply can't keep killing people," I said.

"After you two, there's no one else to kill. I'll be done."

If that remark didn't sink through Geri's state of denial, nothing would.

"You know the two of you will really like the cabin."

"What cabin?" Geri asked.

"The one we're walking to, of course. I checked it out last month. It's for sale, but unfortunately the owners aren't around to give us a tour."

"Who has a cabin out in the middle of nowhere?" Geri asked. She had stopped crying.

"Who knows, but it's not really in the middle of nowhere. We're just approaching it from the rear."

I couldn't see any sign of a cabin ahead of us, but in the darkness it could be out there, and I had no reason to believe Vic was lying. More importantly, I didn't know how close it might be. The urgency of the situation tingled up and down my spine. However, I had to wait until the opportunity came. I didn't know when it would appear, but I knew I would recognize it. Vic might be mentally prepared to kill me, and I had no doubt that he was a damn good shot, but I could hope he didn't have the instincts of a professional.

For much of our trek, a space of four or five yards separated the trees from the path. Finally, I could see the woods close in on the trail a few yards ahead of us. I tugged gently on Geri's arm and looked at her with the corner of my eyes. When she looked back at me, I nodded my head just a fraction to indicate the spot. The bewildered look she gave me didn't make me confident, but I didn't feel we had a choice.

A few steps before the spot where the forest closed in on the path, I looked to my left like I might have heard something. Just as fast I looked back ahead of us but tilted my head slightly to the left. I hoped to appear like I didn't want Vic to know I was looking over there. With any luck, he might be looking to the left when we made our break. My tactic had a lousy downside to it - I wouldn't know if he had taken the bait when we made our move.

My other mistake was to think of it as our move. When the first of the evergreen branches brushed my arm, I bolted into them dragging a half responsive Geri. The darkness immediately surrounded us and branches, large shrubs, and even the larger trees required zigzagging our way into them. The beam of the flashlight caught up with us in pieces, and I started to feel good about the chances until two rapid shots were fired off.

Geri went down and I thought she was hit. I stopped and went down by her side.

"Are you hit?"

"No, but I can't go on. You go!"

"I'm not leaving you!" But I heard the sound of Vic closing in on us, and I knew I had to. I would not get another chance, and by leaving I might be able to do something to help. At a minimum it would make Vic rethink his plans. If I stayed I would be dead.

Fortunately, the flash from the revolver along with our dropping to the ground temporarily confused Vic. He came into the woods after us but off to our right. I moved deeper into the woods, and he must have heard me as the beam of the flashlight caught me before I darted behind a thick clump of bushes.

I took a few more steps and nearly stepped off into dark nothingness. I had to grab the branches of a small cedar to prevent myself from going over. I looked down and couldn't see ground. I heard Vic crashing through the brush behind me. Staying near the edge and behind the cedar, I moved perpendicular to him. A row of thin cedars gave me some cover. I squeezed behind a larger tree. Suddenly, the ground gave out under my feet, and I fell.

Long ago, I read or someone told me that one's chances of surviving a fall from any considerable height goes up significantly if you can land on your feet. That thought raced into my mind the first second I was falling, and during the next second I started to fight my body to get my feet below me. The thump with the ground came in the third second.

The good news came with the quick impact with the ground. I hadn't fallen far enough to pick up any real speed. Additionally, I landed at a spot where leaves, twigs, and other small segments of dead vegetation had collected over the thin layer of dirt that covered the rock ledge.

Bad news also came with the impact. I had no time to get my feet under me, and the impact almost knocked me out. I briefly saw stars. The fall had knocked the wind out of me, and I seemed to be paralyzed. I felt like I was dying, but I didn't. I'd had the wind knocked out of me before and realized that I would just have to suffer a few minutes, fight back the panic, and let time do its healing.

While I lay there, trying to breathe but at the same time stay quiet, I saw the light from the flashlight cut a swath through the darkness. Even though it never reached down to touch me, the light swept by me close enough that I realized I had fallen about ten feet into a crevice not much wider or longer than me. Over the millennium, nature had cut this recess into the side of the cliff.

"You killed him!" Geri screamed.

"Shut up!" I heard the sound of his slapping her, or at least I imagined I did.

"You shot him. I saw him fall." Good ol' Geri lying to protect me.

"Then where is he?"

"Why don't you stand real close to the edge so you can look straight down?"

"So you can push me? You won't get rid of me that easy, Geri."

I didn't hear anything for a few seconds.

"Vic, let me go. I promise I won't tell anyone about you. As your wife, I can't be made to testify."

"We'll talk about that later."

I knew, and she had to know by now that he wouldn't let her go. She would be dead by morning unless I could do something to stop him.

They must have started walking away, because I heard Geri, but the voices were broken.

"…can't just leave him," she said.

"He couldn't……..morning." My mind filled in the blanks. "He couldn't have gone far. I'll look for him in the morning."

My breathing returned to normal about the time I couldn't hear them anymore. I forced myself into a sitting position and studied my surroundings the best I could in the darkness. I had rock walls on three sides of me. I peered over the edge. The ground looked about twenty feet away, straight down.

I stood up and felt for damage. I hurt in a couple of places.
Despite the inch or so of soft debris and dirt, the ledge I landed
on had a rock base. My good shoulder now hurt as much as the
one I had hurt last night. I had a small goose egg on the back of
my head, and my hip on my left side was sore. At least nothing
seemed to be broken, and more importantly, Vic hadn't seen me
down here.

The rock wall had various depressions and ridges, and I
used them to try to climb out. Three times I tried, and three
times I fell back down. I needed more light to see what I was
doing and a better alignment of ridges and crevices. On the
third attempt, I had managed to get my head above the edge
before the ridge I had placed my supporting foot on gave way,
and I slid back down.

Despite the cool night, I found myself sweating profusely.
The low clouds had brought in the warmer than usual
temperatures, but they also ramped up the usually low
humidity for this area. I wanted to hurry, to get to Geri and
somehow rescue her, but I knew I had to calm down and take
the situation one step at a time.

I never doubted that I could climb out, but I needed to get
smart about it. Rather than simply start climbing again, I
looked for a series of spots on the side walls that I could use in
sequence to climb out. I discovered a ledge about four feet high
that stuck out about two inches near the outer edge. It looked
safe enough. If it gave way, and I fell straight back down I
would have about a foot of safety before going over the side to
the rocky ground below. I would have to keep my weight
leaning away from that side.

Unfortunately, taking my time allowed me to start worrying about things I didn't need to think about. As a young teenager climbing the Cliffs of the Neuse in North Carolina, I reached a ledge where I pulled myself up just to discover a copperhead snake. By good fortune, I scared it more than it scared me, and the snake fled away. In late October, at this altitude, all good snakes would be hibernating. At least I hoped that would be the case.

I studied the area above the ledge and saw a jagged piece of rock that would provide support. From there I should be able to grab a low tree limb, a strong bush, something on the ground above to pull myself up.

I stretched and grabbed the jagged rock and used it to support me as I placed my foot on the narrow ledge. Neither crumbled under my weight and I stood there hugging the side of the small cliff and searching with my hands for another place to grip along the top of the rock wall. I found one and continued my climb. My head was now above the ground. I saw a small cedar that gave me something to grasp and use to squirm to the surface. Sharp things made shallow cuts in my hands as I clawed my way up and out. The ground was damp, almost muddy, but I didn't care. I rolled over on my back and breathed in the night air.

Suddenly, the beam of a flashlight lit up my face.

CHAPTER 22

"Jim? Jim? Is that you?"

I immediately recognized the voice, "Sean? What are you doing out here?"

"I saw that guy force you into the car."

"You followed us?"

"I came out on the deck to look for you and saw the guy with the gun then I saw you all drive off. I thought if you got out on the highway, we would never find you, so I decided to follow you."

"Have you called the cops?"

"No. My phone is back in the room being charged."

Damn, I thought.

"Sorry," he said, as though he knew what I was thinking.

"No need to be sorry. We need to hurry now. He's going to kill her if we don't stop him. I need you to head back to the lodge or to somewhere you can call the police."

"I'm not going back."

"What?"

"You go back, and I'll follow them," he said.

"Sean, this isn't safe. Vic has a gun, and we don't. Even if we catch up with them, it'll be a long shot that we can do anything."

"Look, Jim. I didn't do anything last time. I'm not going to cut and run now."

"You're not running, you're going to get help."

"Then you go. They already think I'm a kook. They'd believe you."

We weren't getting anywhere, and time wasn't our ally.

"Okay, let's go see if we can find them."

"The path they were on is right back over here," he said. I followed him to it and realized at the same time that we needed his flashlight. Without it, simply staying on the path would be difficult. Whether we went for help or after Vic, we would both need the same flashlight.

"How did you know where to find me?"

"There wasn't another car on the road. I saw you turn off the main road from way back, and actually drove by the turn to make sure there wasn't another one. There wasn't, so I doubled back and followed you in. Despite your car being behind some bushes, the taillights reflected my headlights. From that point, I followed the only path I could find. I began to think I had made a mistake, when all of a sudden, I heard the gunfire."

"At that point most people would have turned around."

"I couldn't, but I did become more careful. I kept the light pointed downward and watched for you all. I figured one of you had to be carrying a flashlight, too."

I noticed he still kept the light pointing almost straight down.

"I saw the light about the same time I heard the voices. I couldn't catch most of what they were saying, but the gist of it implied you were either dead or missing. I decided to see if I could find you, and almost walked off the cliff just before you popped up."

"You scared me. I thought you were Vic."

"I take it that he's got something to do with the killings."

"You're right. He killed both Cross and Randi."

"Is that the woman?"

"Yeah. He killed them both in some convoluted plan to get his hands on a lot of money."

"How about the woman that's with him? Isn't she his wife?"

"Right again. She needs to die so he can inherit."

"Does he really believe he can get away with all this?" Sean asked.

"Yes."

"You know, I've seen this type situation on television a few times. One of us will need to distract... what's his name again?"

"Vic."

"Yeah, Vic. One of us needs to distract him so the other can get her away from him."

Despite the seriousness of the situation, I had to grin to myself. This was a different side of Sean that I hadn't expected: Sean in charge. I wondered what Colt would think. But despite this bravado and commitment, he needed to know he wasn't going to be in charge.

"Not a bad plan, but we need to catch up with them first. Then we can decide how to proceed, and Sean, we can only count at getting one shot, if that. I need you to let me be in charge of this."

"You've done this before?"

"Yes."

"Are you a cop or in the military?"

"Kind of both for many years."

"Fine, you take the lead, but I'm not going back until the woman is safe."

"Okay."

We followed the trail in silence for a few minutes. I wondered what was going through Sean's mind and kept coming up with redemption. More than that, most likely, but deep down redemption had to be key. A noble cause most of the time, but it, like so many strong emotions, had its drawbacks. I knew a father one time who didn't pay attention to his five year old daughter while shopping at a large hunting and fishing store. An astute security guard noticed a middle aged man carrying a struggling young girl out of the store. The man had his hand over the girl's mouth.

The security guard followed the man to the parking lot where he finally confronted him. At the same time, the radio call came to be on the lookout for a missing girl. The girl was rescued unharmed, the man arrested, and the incident made the nightly news.

The father felt so bad about the whole thing that he went to the other extreme. Two years later at a movie theater, while waiting in the snack line, he turned and saw a man walking his daughter away from him. He had his hand on his daughter's shoulder. Without saying anything the father jumped on the man's back, knocking them both to the ground, and started hitting him with his fists.

By the time they had been pulled apart, the father had broken the man's nose. Turned out the man was his daughter's former school teacher, and he was simply walking her over to say hello to his wife who worked in the small school's front office. Both the adults knew the little girl and were simply saying hello to her. The wife was standing in another snack line nearby.

Good intentions but a bad move. Somehow, I needed to ensure that Sean didn't rush in blindly and get everyone killed.

"Pretty brave of you to take after us like that," I said.

"More necessity than bravery. I had the keys to the car with me, running back inside and telling somebody what had happened to you didn't seem like a smart thing to do. Like I said before, I didn't think anyone would believe me, and even if they did, we would have lost too much time to have any idea which way you went."

I still wasn't sure if he had done the right thing, but having company right now did feel good.

All of a sudden we were out of the forest and in an open area that in the darkness looked sort of like a meadow.

"Turn the light off," I whispered. Once he did, I pointed ahead of us. "Look. I see one, two, …. three houses."

"They look like cabins," he corrected me.

It didn't matter what they were. "I think I can see a light on in the closest one and the one further down to our right."

"You think that's where they are?" he asked.

"One of these three has to be the cabin he was leading us to." Despite the darkness the cabins stood out against the native background.

"Would he use a light if the cabin was supposed to be vacant?"

"He might. I don't think he had enough lead on us to have gotten to the furthest house yet. I can't see anyone walking around with a flashlight out there. Although like us, he may have turned his flashlight off when they got to this spot," I said. I instinctively squatted down and surveyed the area ahead of us again.

Sean followed my lead and knelt down next to me. "Think they're still out there somewhere?" he asked looking around.

"Maybe, but I can't see them. Can you?"

"No. My guess is that they're in that house right there."

He indicated the closest one.

"You mean the cabin right there," I said grinning at him.

"Yeah, cabin. What do we want to do?"

"We go there, quietly and carefully. We either find them or someone else. If it's someone else, we have them call the Sheriff. If it's them, we'll have to come up with a plan."

"Sounds good," Sean said.

"Remember Sean, nothing rash."

"Okay."

We started our approach to the house. It looked about three hundred yards away. A short par four, I thought. In the darkness, we soon found ourselves off the trail. It may have ended or meandered in a different direction, but we took a direct route to the closest house. I checked my watch. Ten o'clock.

"Are we going to look in the windows?"

"Yes."

"What if they have a dog?" he asked.

"We'll soon find out."

"You know if it's not them, but some other family, and they see us looking in their windows, can't we get into trouble ourselves?"

Obviously, Sean was getting nervous. I stopped and grabbed his arm. My grip was firm, but I didn't jerk him to a stop. I didn't want to get him any more agitated than he was.

"Would you rather wait here?" I asked.

"No, no. I'm just thinking out loud."

"Anything that brings the police out here will be to our advantage. Don't worry, we'll be very careful."

I felt like saying that if he wanted to worry about something, he could worry about being seen by the occupants, whoever they might be, and having our heads blown off before they took the time to call the police. Very few people who live in the country, and especially out here in the semi-wilderness, have much sympathy for prowlers.

We were only about twenty yards from the back of the cabin when the light went out. We both froze. I looked around to confirm what I already knew. The backyard provided nothing to hide behind, no big bush, no tree, no shed, just an open field.

It felt like suicide at the time, but I ran toward the cabin and braced myself flat against the wall between the window and the back door. Sean impressed me by following my lead. He stood, pressed against the wall of the house on the other side of the door. I could sense his fear, but maybe that was my own.

No sounds came from the house. I counted to fifty before I moved. When I did, I slid my body to the edge of the window and peered through it. Partially shut blinds blocked most of my view, and the darkness didn't help, but I could make out a few pieces of furniture. I saw no sign of life.

I looked over at Sean. He had already moved down to the window on his side. He stared into it, and I waited silently for him to finish. When he did, he turned toward me and shook his head. I moved over to the door. It appeared to be a solid piece of wood without even a peep hole. I gently checked the door knob and found it locked.

Sean moved in close to me.

"What's next?" he asked.

That had been running through my mind, too. Why were we here? Why didn't we run back to his car and drive somewhere for help? I knew why, but I didn't know if I had made the right decision. If we had gone back we would have lost time, maybe an hour or two, and we would have had less of an idea than we had now as to where they could be. It was the same reasoning Sean used when he jumped into his car and followed us.

The best idea would be for us to find one of these houses occupied by someone other than Vic and Geri and call the police from there. But which one? If we could see Vic or Geri through a window, we could sprint to another house. But until we did, we could just as easily run to the one where they were.

"Let's see if we can find another window to look through."

He nodded, and we both crept along the edge of the house. We went around the corner and up the side. The only window on this side was near the front of the house, but it was covered on the inside by what looked like heavy curtains.

I looked up and saw Sean already peering around the front corner.

"Sean," I whispered, but he disappeared around the corner. As he did, a light came on.

CHAPTER 23

Sean nearly flew back around the corner of the house. For a second I thought he might take off running. I grabbed his sleeve, and he squatted down behind the single small bush that some landscaper thought would be the perfect adornment for this corner. It didn't give us much cover as we both huddled there.

"A security light," he said with his voice kept low. I could see the beads of sweat on his forehead.

"That's why I called for you. You can't just rush off."

We remained still for about thirty seconds.

"The people inside may not have noticed, or they may have checked all the windows and just assumed the light was set off by an animal."

"They could think you're following them," Sean said.

"If it's them, if they noticed, and if they think I'm still alive. Let's go back around to the other side and check the far windows."

We moved slowly and kept close to the ground. Sean followed my lead. Two smaller windows broke the monotony of the wall on this side of the cabin. Unfortunately both windows were covered with curtains. A very small gap in the curtains allowed me to see that one of the rooms was a bedroom, but other than the corner of a bed and a small, empty area beyond, I saw nothing.

"We'll have to try the front door," I said.

"How? Won't that be dangerous?"

"Yeah, but I have an idea. First though, I need you to go back around and position yourself behind that bush again."

"Then what?"

I explained my idea to him. He liked it.

I waited at my corner. I put just enough of my head out to see. While I waited the light went out. I hadn't timed the light but I figured it had only been on for a minute or two. I saw Sean wave a hand at me from the far corner. The light went back on.

"Damn," I said to myself, but I knew it didn't matter because it would have gone on with my next step. I ran to the front door, found the button for the door bell and pushed it twice. I also hit the door once for good luck and then ran back to my corner.

My plan was simple. If Vic answered the door, I would say something to get his attention. Something that would let him know I was still alive and that I knew where he was. I would then take off at a full sprint toward the far cabin. If he ran after me, Sean would go in, grab Geri, and get her out. If he had to, he would carry her out and head in the opposite direction. If Vic didn't go after me, Sean would stay in the shadows and watch the house to see if Vic left before the police arrived. I didn't suggest that he follow them if they did leave, but I expected that he would.

There was a flaw in my planning that I tried not to think about, but when no one came to the door I realized I should have given it more consideration. After about a minute of waiting, I saw Sean crawl to the front window. He peered in and then looked at me and shook his head. I crawled to the matching window on my side of the front door and looked in. No sign of life.

"We saw a light on in this house. Someone has to be in there," he said after he came to me.

The idea that the light may have been on a timer and that there really was no one inside started making sense. Why would Vic have turned all the lights out? We didn't see any indication of a flashlight being used in the house as we approached it or after the light went out.

"Maybe not," I said, hoping I sounded more confident than I was.

"Should we go to another cabin?"

"I'm going to break into this cabin. If no one is inside I'll use the phone to call the sheriff's office. We need to get them out here."

"What if someone is inside? You could get yourself killed."

"You can watch. If I do get shot by Vic in there, run to another house and get help. If I get shot but it's not Vic, yell at them to call the police. Tell them what's going on and that they need to get the sheriff out here. Either way, don't worry about me. It'll be too late at that point."

"Come on," I said. I went around back. I didn't want to be the one standing in the light if any shooting started. A light mist had started falling, or perhaps the clouds simply had come down to us.

I found a rock about the size of a baseball and used it to smash a hole in the window just above the single latch. I felt like the sound of the breaking glass could be heard for miles. I reached in, unlocked the latch, and then slid the bottom window up. Before I entered, I looked through the blinds, but still saw no signs of life. I felt a little more confident that no one was in the cabin.

After brushing off the few pieces of glass I could see, I crawled through the open window. I moved quickly to the far wall before I paused and listened again. Still no noise to indicate anyone else might be there. I moved as silently but as quickly as I could from room to room. The place was empty. I found the lamp plugged into a timer on the kitchen counter.

I turned on a couple of overhead lights and looked for a phone. I shouldn't have been surprised by not finding one. More people were moving away from land line phones every day. It only made sense that if someone used this cabin for weekends or the occasional vacation that they may not want to bother with a phone.

To me, though, it was like another punch in the gut. Time wasted and nothing to show for it. They may not have even stopped in this cluster of cabins. For all I knew there might be a dozen more cabins a half mile away.

"Jim," Sean called from another room. He had not waited outside like we had planned, but I guessed that once I started turning on lights he figured no one else was in the cabin.

"In here," I said.

"Any telephone?"

"No."

He sat down in a cushioned chair and had a frustrated look on his face.

"What now?"

"We move to the next cabin. We either find them or find a way to get in touch with the sheriff's office."

"Think we'll be too late for Geri?"

"No," I said without conviction. It struck me that this was the first time he had used her name.

I closed and locked the window despite it being broken. After turning off the lights we went out the back door, locking it too. The house to our left looked a couple hundred yards away. The one to our right appeared to be about twice as far. I looked again to try to see another one. I didn't see any more, but they could have been out there hidden in or behind the trees. A dirt road ran in an arc in front of the three cabins.

We hadn't seen any light in the closer of the two cabins, but that didn't mean much.

"Should we run?" Sean asked.

"Better not. We might miss something if we do, and we'll make too much noise breathing once we get there." I didn't blame him. I wanted this to get over quickly, too.

This time we followed the dirt road until we were close to the cabin. We were about thirty yards from the right, front corner when I saw what looked like a small light flicker through the front window. Then it went away.

I left the road and hurried to the corner of the house. I didn't know if Sean saw anything, but he followed me. Once there, I looked for security lights and didn't see any. A small section of roofing, more decorative than functional, covered the front entrance and had a single light recessed into it. The light was not on. I crawled over and peered into the front window. This window was much larger than the two front windows at the previous cabin, and it was the only window facing the front yard.

I saw furniture but no people. More importantly, however, I saw light coming from below a closed door to an adjoining room. I studied the interior of the cabin. The large front room served as the family or living room. A kitchen occupied one far end of the large open area, and a short hallway led back to one or two other rooms.

"What do you see?"

I stood up and walked to the far side of the cabin. The side from where the light seemed to originate.

"Nothing yet," I said.

He paused at the window and looked in making no effort to conceal himself.

"Look," Sean said.

I turned and saw he was looking in the direction of the far house. The one we had not been to yet. A car had just pulled in front of it. Its headlights went out while we watched. Two people got out of the car and entered the house. The distance and the darkness made it impossible to tell anything more than it was two people, and we only knew that because the light from the car indicated that two car doors had been opened and two figures got out.

"Why don't you run over there and get them to call the police?" I whispered.

"Why don't you run over there instead?   I want to be part of this."

"Let's hope we both don't regret what we're doing."

We continued around the side of the cabin. A window near the middle of the side wall definitely belonged to a room where the light was on inside. Unfortunately, a heavy curtain covered the entire window and blocked our view of what or who was inside. I moved to the next window, near the back corner of the cabin. It also had a curtain hanging inside, but there didn't appear to be any light on inside of the room.

We checked out the rear of the cabin, but the only window on it came off what I believed to be the kitchen and was too high off the ground to look through. No light shone through the window, so I didn't think it mattered anyway.   The cabin did have a solid back door. I checked it and found it to be locked.

"Same game plan?" Sean asked.

"Yeah," I said, and we moved around to the front of the cabin.

To my surprise, the light in the interior room had been turned off.

"The light's out," Sean said.

We crouched at the corner of the window for about thirty seconds waiting for any sign of movement from inside.   When we didn't get any, I told Sean to move to the far corner and that we were going to do the same thing we did at the last house.

He went across the front of the house and positioned himself.   I approached the front door, and as I did, I thought I heard the sound of a door closing. I peaked back through the window and saw nothing.   I rang the doorbell.

I jumped back to my corner and waited. Again, nothing happened. I began to dislike my plan. If someone was in there waiting for us, and particularly if that someone was Vic, then we were really asking to be shot dead as soon as we entered.

I leaned back against the wall to consider the options. That far house was looking better and better. We might not be anywhere near Vic and Geri, or they might just be inside. Sean motioned at me, but I didn't understand what he was trying to indicate. I looked behind me as a precaution but didn't see anything.

I waved Sean over and he came.

"What's up? I asked.

"I heard something."

"So did I. The sound of a door being shut," I said.

"Me, too, and then I think I heard voices, or at least a voice."

"Obviously someone is inside," I said.

"Do we still want to go in?" he asked.

Good question, I thought, as my feet were getting colder, too. Then I heard the voice.

"That's coming from out back," I said.

We moved in unison to the back corner of the cabin. There, maybe thirty to forty yards away, we saw a man carrying something heavy over his shoulder. That something appeared to be a somebody.

"Quit wiggling or I'll put you down and shoot you right here," the man snarled. The voice belonged to Vic.

"What do we do?" Sean whispered so lightly I almost couldn't hear him.

"He doesn't know you're out here. Let me distract him and

see if I can get him away from Geri. She must still be alive."

"Okay."

"If it works, once he's away from her be quick. Grab her and run, and be quiet."

"I will."

"Stay here until it's time."

"Okay."

Leaving him there, I went around the house to the other side. Vic had not noticed us. He must have left the house seconds before I rang the door bell. In the dark, it had become harder to see him, but I could still just make him out. I wondered where he was taking Geri. There didn't seem to be anything ahead of him for some distance.

I took off on a run again paralleling him, but moving slightly away from him as I came alongside. He didn't hear me, not because I'm a silent runner, but rather he was struggling and mumbling to himself or Geri as he walked. I couldn't understand him, but I could hear him as I got closer. I stopped about forty yards to his left. As I did, I saw a small lake appear out of the darkness about another twenty yards in front of us.

"Vic!" I shouted. "Give it up. I've called the cops. They know what's up. There's no reason for any more killing."

He stopped and dropped Geri. She hit the ground with a thump.

I had picked the distance because in the dark hitting a stationary target with a hand gun at forty plus yards is a challenge, and I planned to be a moving target. I saw his arm come up, so I moved a few more paces away from him.

He flicked on the flashlight. The faint beam barely lit me up, but I moved to my left toward the lake. I didn't want to make this too easy on him. I thought he would talk to me, say something about his predicament, but he didn't. The flashlight started bobbing up and down and I knew he was coming at me. I turned and ran as fast as I could toward the woods. With a forty yard head start, I thought my odds of beating him there were very good. He didn't look in any better shape than me, and he wasn't being chased by some idiot with a gun.

I wanted to turn and look back, but I knew I couldn't look away from the ground. In the darkness it was already too easy to trip over something. I estimated the tree line to be around a hundred yards away. I sprinted and waited for the sound of gunfire behind me.

CHAPTER 24

For some reason, Vic didn't fire until I reached the tree line. I guess he had hoped I would fall or that he could outrun me, but either way I'm not complaining. His first shot slammed into a tree at least three feet to my right as I passed it. He fired a second shot. It also missed. I had to slow down once I entered the forest, but I still moved as quickly as I dared for a few seconds before turning ninety degrees to my right toward the lake. I moved as quietly as I could another ten to fifteen yards and hid behind the base of a large tree. A thick patch of smaller bushes had grown up along the trunk.

I saw the broken beams of light emanating from the flashlight and being shredded by the underbrush. I couldn't see Vic. I don't think he entered the tree line by more than a yard or so and was now searching the area with his light.

"What? Damn!" or words to that effect roared out of Vic's mouth and then the light disappeared.

I remained motionless. I couldn't see anything beyond a few yards away. The forest swallowed what little light made it this far. For ten to fifteen seconds, everything seemed eerily quiet.

"I'm going to kill you!" Vic yelled at someone. It sounded like he had returned to the spot where he had dropped Geri, but he shouted loud enough that I heard him. I hoped Sean and Geri were long gone.

I moved toward the voice, and stopped at the edge of the trees. I saw movement in the distance.

"Give it up Vic!" I shouted. "It's over."

He didn't respond to me, but he must have heard me. I saw the beam of the flashlight swing back around and point in my direction. The weak beam of light would be ineffective at this distance. The light moved toward the lake, and I saw that it came to rest on a small canoe on the bank. It flicked off, and for a moment, I saw nothing. Then something, I assumed Vic, moved in the distant darkness toward the cabin we had all just come from. Surely Sean wouldn't have stopped there, but either way, he was on his own now. Our element of surprise was over. A head on assault on Vic now would be suicide. Even Sean had to realize that.

Besides, Sean knew that Vic didn't know he was out here. Vic would assume that Geri got to her feet and hobbled off on her own. The way he had carried her, I was sure he had bound both her hands and feet. He would conclude that she couldn't have gone far.

The ground fell off slightly by the lake, so I stayed close to the bank to prevent his seeing my silhouette in the darkness. I knew the lake blocked one of my avenues of escape, but I wanted to check out the canoe. Actually, I wanted to do more than check it out. Vic planned to do something with it, of that I was certain. He had been heading right to it when I surprised him. Whether he intended to dump Geri out in the middle of the lake or use it to escape, I thought messing with his plans one more time couldn't hurt.

The canoe looked to be in good shape, and a new paddle rested against one of its benches. I looked around, and not seeing anyone coming, I slid the canoe onto the lake. I climbed in as soon as my shoes made contact with the water and started paddling. The canoe moved smoothly through the dark water. I had to fight the urge to look back despite the hairs on my neck trying their best to urge me to hurry up.

The lake didn't look that large. Of course, at any far point, a small part of it could feed into another expanse. I aimed at a point on the shore about one hundred and fifty yards away. It took me on a diagonal to my right and to a spot about ten yards inside the forest. During daylight this small lake had to be picturesque framed against the trees. In the darkness, however, everything appeared ominous.

The canoe cut through the water without a sound. When I neared the shore, I let the canoe drift in. The small boat ground against the small rocks and dirt. I stood up and walked to the front of the bow. As I stepped over the front bench, I saw something that I hadn't noticed before. I must have seen it, because it wasn't small, but in the darkness it hadn't registered.

I leaned down to inspect it: a round, flat object about an inch thick with a hole in the middle. Even in the darkness I thought I could read the number 25 written on it. I felt the raised number with my fingers. Twenty five pounds of weight normally found on one end or the other of a weightlifter's bar. In this case, the thin wire attached to it would have been wrapped around Geri, and the weight would have taken Geri down to the bottom of the lake. The thought sent shivers through me.

I pulled the boat onto shore and into the trees. I heard a noise to my right and immediately crouched behind some bushes. He couldn't have followed me without the use of his flashlight, and I would've noticed that. Nothing moved nearby, and the silence finally gave me the nerve to move. My coming onto shore must have spooked a deer or other wild animal.

Still, I spent close to a minute moving the short distance from the canoe to the edge of the trees. Once there, I studied the open space as far as I could see. The third cabin, the one we hadn't checked out, appeared all lit up. Other than that, the rest of the world looked dark and lifeless. I hoped the lights on at the cabin meant that Sean and Geri made it there. The people in the cabin would have called the Sheriff, and I doubted that Vic would attack them there.

Where would he be? I hated staying in the trees. For the first time that night, the cold had successfully fought its way through my jacket and my adrenalin. I started shivering and felt miserable. I leaned against a nearby tree and waited.

Fortunately, I didn't have to wait that long. After about ten minutes, a vehicle with flashing lights pulled up to the far cabin. I fought the urge to start running at it. About five minutes later an ambulance, followed almost immediately by two more sheriff's vehicles, pulled in next to the cabin. A spotlight scanned the area around the cabin. Then the vehicle with the spotlight on it moved slowly in my direction.

It seemed to take an eternity for the cruiser to get close enough to me for the spotlight to do any good. I walked out of my hiding spot and held my hands up to indicate I posed no threat. I didn't know how jittery the deputies might be. It took a lot longer than I expected for the spotlight to finally hit me. When it did, the vehicle stopped, and so did I.

"Approach the light and keep your hands in the air," a deputy spoke through the car's loudspeaker system.

Silhouetted by the spotlight, I felt a little naked. If Vic was still around and wanted to take a potshot at me, there was nothing like a lit up target in the darkness. Granted, if he had any sense, he'd be long gone by now, but after what he had already done, I couldn't give him too much credit in the common sense department.

"Stop right there," the speaker roared again, too loud at this short of a distance. I stopped about fifteen paces from the car.

A deputy approached me from the other side of the sedan.

"Turn around," she ordered.

"I'm Jim West. I'm the good guy," I said, but I still turned around.

She did a quick frisk looking for any obvious weapons, then grabbed my arms and cuffed me.

"Get in the car," she ordered. "We'll get this straightened out soon enough."

I climbed into the back seat, and a moment later we were speeding back to the cabin with all the lights on.

"Are my friends safe?" I asked.

Neither of them answered me. We pulled in front of the cabin at the same time another sheriff's vehicle arrived. This one brought Detective Bruno. The female deputy from the car that held me captive walked up to him. I saw a big grin appear on his face early in the conversation. He looked over in my direction. His grin seemed to get even larger. They both approached the car.

"Who's this nefarious criminal you captured?" Bruno asked while opening my door.

"Not funny," I said.

"You can release him, Polly. That is unless you want to keep him - he is single."

He caught Polly off guard with his comment. She must not have known that Deputy Bruno considered us buddies. Plus, she may not have thought his comment was especially appropriate. However, she did help me out of the car and removed the handcuffs.

"Just following procedure, you know," she said quietly.

I wondered if she didn't want Bruno to hear her.

"So Mr. Victor Schutte is our killer. You know, he was my top pick of the litter," Bruno remarked.

"I'll walk him inside, Detective."

"Good, good," Bruno mumbled.

I had the feeling then that Bruno may have had a few drinks before arriving at the scene.

"I think I'll walk around and see if he's still out there somewhere," Bruno said.

My deputy escort stopped in her tracks and made eye contact with her partner, who now stood outside the sheriff's vehicle he had been driving. She motioned with her head, and her partner nodded.

"Let me go with you, Detective," her partner suggested to Bruno.

The two of them walked away, and we continued inside. The house bubbled with activity. One deputy talked on the phone, a woman with pretty straight grey hair, maybe a few years older than me, poured coffee in cups set on a tray, two emergency service technicians were trying to check out Geri, and Geri had a death grip on Sean's right arm. Sean saw me and smiled. His eyes and smile screamed "Redemption!"

I gave him a thumbs-up, and he returned the gesture.

"Please, let go of him and relax, so we can make sure you're okay," one of them said to Geri.

"I don't want to let go of him. He saved my life out there." She turned to face Sean and then rested her head on his shoulder. If they were cats, one or both of them would have been purring.

I could see that Geri's wrists and legs above her ankles were red. I guessed the wounds came from duct tape or something similar used to bind her legs and arms.

Another deputy sat at a table and wrote notes on a sheet of paper. A man walked out of an adjoining room and went directly into the kitchen. He looked at me as he passed, but his eyes lingered a little longer on Polly. I didn't see any recognition by either, so I figured he was the man of the house.

"You okay?" Sean asked me.

"Yeah, just a little cold."

"Do you know where he is?"

"No, but hopefully nowhere near here," I said.

"Let's hold off on the conversation until we've had a chance to talk," Deputy Polly said.

"Okay."

She led me to the far side of the small table where the deputy was writing.

"Now what can you tell me about what happened tonight?" she asked once we were both seated.

"The whole story?"

"Yes."

I started at the point where I saw Vic and Geri arguing by their car and explained that I knew he wanted to leave tonight, but that she wanted to wait until tomorrow. When he became violent, I walked up to them simply to calm things down. When I mentioned the revolver appearing in Vic's hand, the deputy doing the writing put his pen down and started listening. From then until I stopped talking about thirty minutes later, they both just listened and asked few questions.

More deputies arrived and left, and I had two cups of very good coffee before the interview ended. At that point, I led the two deputies interviewing me to the canoe, pointed out where the canoe had been before I had taken it, and pointed out the two cabins Sean and I visited. I made sure they understood that Vic had spent some time in the one cabin. I admitted to breaking a window at the other cabin in order to gain access, but they didn't seem interested. We saw no sign of Vic.

We returned to the cabin. Geri's grip on Sean hadn't loosened a bit, but if it bothered him, I couldn't tell. The two medical service personnel had departed, and I realized that I hadn't seen the ambulance out front. More deputies were in the house, but I didn't see Bruno. A deep voice boomed behind me. I turned and saw the Sheriff. He held a large mug of coffee in his hands.

"Everybody but Smitty and Polly outside and start looking. I imagine he's miles from here by now, but let's get going. You know your search areas. Let's go."

The place emptied. He looked at me and smiled.

"I hear you had an exciting night," he said.

"That's right, Sheriff, but I'm glad it's over."

"Why don't you have a seat over there with your friends? Polly, Smitty, you two with me in the kitchen."

I hadn't talked to Smitty, but I believed he was the deputy who had been interviewing Sean and Geri. I sat down on the couch next to Sean. The couch was barely large enough for three adults. Fortunately Sean and Geri weren't taking up much space, so I could stretch out.

"I'm glad you're safe, Jim. I really thought you went over that cliff. Wasn't it great that Sean came along and saved us both?"

I didn't quite remember Sean's role being any more significant than mine. After all, I put myself out as a target to draw Vic away from her, not Sean. Yet, I knew in the end it didn't matter who she wanted to credit for her rescue.

"Absolutely," I said.

I looked at Sean. His eyes were focused on Geri, not me. I'm not sure he even heard what she said. Geri rested her head on Sean's shoulder again and shut her eyes. Sean rested his head on top of hers and shut his eyes. I had taken a seat on the couch so I could talk to Sean. Now I felt like I was intruding in their space.

I moved to the only chair in the living room, an old rocker with a flowery cushion. I think both Sean and Geri had fallen asleep, and I almost had before Polly and Smitty came out of the kitchen.

"Okay you all, let's get you back to the lodge," Polly said.

I liked Deputy Polly. She was all business. I couldn't help but wonder what she was like in her civilian life. With her uniform, jacket and hat on, I couldn't tell much about her, but she came across as very competent.

"How about my car?" Sean asked.

"We have that area staked out. We'd prefer to leave it undisturbed, at least until the morning," Smitty said.

The three of us piled into the back seat of the same Sheriff's sedan that I had been in earlier. This time Polly drove us. I tried some small talk on the way back, but Sean and Geri didn't have much interest in conversation, at least not with me. I put my head back and tried to get some sleep, but I had too much on my mind.

I tried to put myself in Vic's place. Where would he, could he go? He would most likely be captured within twenty four hours. However, until he was, I figured Geri might be in danger. There had been deputies in and around the lodge for the past couple of days. I imagined keeping one there for another day to watch Geri shouldn't be much of a problem for them.

A funny thought popped into my mind. It had only been a few hours ago she had insinuated that if she became afraid she might come to me, or was that Randi who had said that? Tonight, Geri had a new hero. Good for both of them, I thought.

The trip back took longer than the drive out because the road from the cabins went in the wrong direction for a few miles before it intersected with the main road. I looked at my watch. It surprised me that it was only a little after midnight. It looked like I could still get in a good six hours or so of sleep. Tomorrow would be another long day, but I was definitely going home tomorrow.

Despite all the excitement, no one had briefed the lodge. The bar was empty, the dining room door shut and the lone clerk at the reception counter looked half asleep. Our arrival, along with the two deputies, livened him up.

"Evening. Is everything all right?" he asked.

"Now it is," Geri spoke first.

We walked by the receptionist and headed for our rooms. Polly escorted Geri but only detached her from Sean after the two had agreed to spend the night together in his room. Geri said she didn't want to spend another night in her old room, the one that she had shared with Vic. Polly had suggested the lodge could give her a new room, but Geri insisted she would feel safer with Sean.

The remaining deputy didn't know which one of us he should escort to our rooms. I suggested Sean as that was where Geri would be shortly anyway. It worked, and I returned to my room alone. I did inspect it, even though I couldn't imagine Vic heading back here. I was alone and safe. I showered and went to bed. Despite all the excitement, I fell asleep soon after my head hit the pillow.

CHAPTER 25

The ringing of the lodge phone awoke me at seven thirty.

"Yeah," I managed to croak into the phone.

"Good morning, Jim. This is Randall. Get your butt down here, and I'll buy you some breakfast."

"Someone's in a good mood," I said to kill time while I tried to remember if I had met a Randall recently.

"Why wouldn't I be? We've got the case solved. Both of them."

Oh yeah, I remembered a Randall, a Detective Randall Bruno.

"Did you find Vic?" I asked.

"Not yet, but it's only a matter of time. He's probably out freezing his butt off in the mountains right about now, but come on down. I do need to talk to you."

"Give me five minutes," I said and hung up.

Detective Bruno sat at a table in the dining room by himself with two cups of steaming coffee placed in front of him. The rest of the dining room was still empty.

He stood when I approached with a big grin on his face.

"I understand you had a scary night last night," he said.

"You were there for part of it."

"Only a few minutes. I shouldn't have come out at all, but I had to.   My neighbors celebrated their twentieth wedding anniversary last night, and I'd had too much to drink. But when I heard the news, I had to come out."

I imagined someone whisked Bruno away before the Sheriff showed up, but I didn't say anything. Bruno handed me the second cup of coffee and we sat down. The strong coffee helped rid my head of the remnants of fatigue, a result of being awakened before I was ready.

A waiter showed up, and we both ordered the full "Pecos" breakfast. Once I had ordered, I realized how hungry I was.

"So, what can I do for you this morning?"

"A few answers are all that I need."

"Fire away."

"We have your story, Bettes' story, and Mrs. Schutte's. You say that you went out from the lodge to the car where the Schuttes were arguing because you believed that she might be in some sort of danger."

"Yes, that's right."

"Did you and she have any prearranged agreement that you would watch out for her?" he asked.

"No.   I had talked to her earlier in the day about her disagreement with her husband. I knew there were some bad feelings, so when I saw him slap her, I simply had to step in to see if I could diffuse the situation. It kind of backfired on me."

"You hadn't decided by then that he was our killer?"

"No, at least not consciously. He had to be on everyone's short list, but at the time, I don't remember thinking that I'd better get out there to help her because he's the murderer."

"And you had no agreement with Sean Bettes that he was to watch your back?"

"No, none at all."

"So everything happened as you all have said: that each of you acted independently based on what you witnessed at the time."

"Yes." I almost added that there actually was a lot more to it. All of us had complicated motivations. None of us reacted simply because of what we saw, but I didn't want to get into all that, and I doubted that any of it would interest him. Bettes' emotional baggage could be an hour long discussion by itself.

"Didn't any of you think about calling me first?"

"I would've, but Vic took my phone immediately after pulling the gun on me."

"You know your stunt almost got you killed."

"Hey, come on, give me a break. You would've done the same thing."

"Yeah, maybe so." He paused for a minute and looked around. "In all your contact with Schutte or any of them did you get any feeling for where he may have fled to? That is if he isn't still hiding behind a tree out there?"

"No, none at all."

Our breakfast arrived, and Bruno's personality improved immediately.

"Oh, look at this," he said. "Let's dig in, and enough about this investigation for now."

"Amen to that."

We both attacked the plates set in front of us.

"You know, this might be the biggest case we've seen in this county in the last decade. I have to say that I'm certainly happy it's been resolved."

So much for not talking about the investigation, I thought.

"Well, you still have to catch him."

"Of course, but it's no longer one of those unknown subject cases. The DA, the Sheriff, everybody agrees Schutte is our guy. Yes-sir-ree, it's a good day in the Pecos." Bruno focused his attention back on his breakfast, and I did the same.

I saw Bev peek her head around the door to the dining room. She saw me, smiled, and mouthed "later" or something like that. I wondered what brought her here so early. I started to excuse myself when Sean entered the dining room.

"There's Sean now."

Detective Bruno had to turn around to see him. Sean took a table not far from us and nodded a "Good morning" at us.

"Oh, good. He was the next person I wanted to talk to," Bruno said to me. "Do you mind if I move over to his table? I think we covered everything we'd wanted to double check with you."

"By all means."

"And, I'll get the check. I owe you at least that."

For about one micro-second I considered arguing with him over the bill, but he was right. He owed me.

He took one last bite of toast, got up, and went over to Sean's table taking his coffee with him. Sean appeared to be in a good mood. He stood up, met Bruno as he approached the table, and motioned for Bruno to join him.

When our server returned and refilled my coffee cup, I told

him that Detective Bruno would be paying for our breakfast. I took my coffee and went out into the lobby to look for Bev. I saw her bent over behind the bar going through one of the cabinets.

"Kind of early to be opening the bar," I said.

"Oh Jim, I'm glad you're up this morning."

"What do you mean?" I asked as we talked across the counter to each other.

"I wanted so much to talk to you, and I'm leaving."

"You're leaving?" I asked.

"Yes, but first, I wanted to ask you what happened last night? The word is that you, Mrs. Schutte, and Sean Bettes discovered that her husband killed those two people. I heard that he almost killed all of you, too."

"It's a long story, but we're all fine," I said in hopes of avoiding the full story.

"Tell me something about it."

I summarized the events of the prior night the best I could. She had a few questions, but for the most part she let me tell the story.

"Wow, that's fantastic," she said when I finished. "Do they have any idea where Vic might be now?"

"No. Everyone's best guess is that he's hiding out back in the mountains somewhere. I imagine they'll catch him in the next day or so."

"I hope so. You don't think he'll come back here, do you?"

"No. He'd be crazy to do so. I think the sheriff will leave a deputy or two here until Mrs. Schutte leaves anyway."

"Oh yeah, her. I bet you're really her hero now." Her eyes

couldn't conceal the fact she was playing with me.

"You would think so," I said in mock disappointment, "but she seems to be smitten with Sean. After all, he's the one that literally picked her up off the ground and carried her off to safety, while I had the easy job of being a zigzagging target for Vic to chase and shoot at."

She reached over and placed a hand on mine. "You are a brave man, Jim West. I think she's smitten with the wrong hero."

"Yeah, me too. Now tell me your story."

"While you were out having all the fun last night, I decided to call an old friend. His name is Eric Brooks. Years back, he and I became good friends. It was before I moved here. He used to pass through on business, so I would see him every few months. It wasn't one of my normal relationships with men."

"What do you mean?"

"Look, to say I've been a little rough around the edges would put it mildly. I think I bored you with my life's story that first day you were here. Well, this relationship was different. Whenever he was in town, we did things together, but he never made a move on me. At first, I thought it was refreshing, but after a while I wondered what was up."

"Like maybe he wasn't into women?"

"Yes and no. I knew he had a wife, so I thought that might be it, too. But I also worried that maybe he really didn't find me attractive. Stupid me. I set him up one night."

"Set him up?"

"Yes, and to this day I'm not proud of it."

"What happened?"

"I made an excuse to have him over to my apartment for dinner, plowed him with wine and seduced him."

"And?" I asked, now hooked and wanting to hear the rest of the story.

"It was a great night. He told me he loved me. I felt like a young girl in love again myself."

"So?"

"That was the last time I saw him. He sent me two dozen roses and a long letter. He apologized for his behavior. He said he should've known better, that from the first day he met me he knew if he kept seeing me he would fall in love with me. He said despite knowing better he couldn't stay away. Did I tell you he was married?"

"Uh-oh," I said, even though she had already told me that.

"It was my fault. As usual I was only thinking of myself. I don't blame him. I knew he was married and like I said, looking back, you don't have to be a rocket scientist to see that his relationship with me wasn't motivated by his desire to cheat on his wife. I encouraged him. Hell, I pushed him across that line."

"Don't be so hard on yourself."

"I've always felt like I betrayed our relationship."

"That's silly. Believe me. He probably happily remembers that night. He just had a choice to make, and he chose not to leave his family. So getting back to your story, what happened on the phone call last night?"

"About a year ago, I received a letter from him. I was surprised it got to me here at all, but the person who is renting the same place I used to live at knew someone who knew where I live now. Anyway, to make a long story short, the letter arrived here, and in it, Eric told me his wife had passed away about a year earlier from cancer."

"See - he hadn't lost interest in you."

She smiled, and I couldn't help but be happy for her.

"The letter was pretty simple asking me how I was doing and telling me a little about his life on the ranch. At the end, he did say he would like to stay in touch."

"Did you write him back?" I asked.

"No. I had just started my relationship with Rick and felt pretty happy about my life. I've never been good at making good decisions, Jim."

"So, are you going to go see him?"

"Yes. I'm leaving today."

"That quick?"

"Yes. Last night Rick gave me hell for not being nicer to his wife."

"You're kidding me."

"No. When I was driving home last night, I decided that I had to leave. I guess I won't actually drive away for another day or two, but I'm quitting this place today and will leave as soon as I can get the U-haul filled."

"I think you're doing the right thing, Bev."

"I'm so worried about whether I can do it."

"Do what?"

"Settle down, be a normal person, not screw things up."

"Not worried about if he'll want you to stay?" I didn't mean it the way it sounded, but she took my comment in stride.

"A little, but I can handle that. I can appreciate his deciding that I'm not for him. In fact, it seems that's the role I normally have: the extra."

"Oh come on," I said.

"I don't mean to sound so morbid, but his telling me it's been a nice visit, but don't I have somewhere to go, I can handle. Of course I'll be disappointed, but I can handle rejection. It's whether or not I can control myself that scares me. He's a good man, Jim."

"So you've told me."

"If I get there and things go good and I end up staying--"

"Getting married?" I interrupted.

"That's up to him, I don't care. But, what if I get there and things start off great, and in a few weeks, a few months, I end up throwing myself at the first cowboy that looks good in jeans?"

"Why would you do that?"

"I don't know. I just do."

"We're all a little older now, and a little wiser. You may find out that you're not as bad of a person as you think you are."

"I hope so, Jim, because I'm going up there as soon as I can, and I do want to make it work."

"Then make it work. You simply must do your best. Remember, it's as important to you as it is to him. Be yourself, unless you're around some cowboy in tight jeans."

"I will," she said. "I'm so happy I met you Jim. If it doesn't work with Eric, I'll come looking for you."

"No way. You'll make it work. Don't start thinking of a fallback position. If you want this to work, you've got to be committed to this."

"I know," she said.

We talked a little while longer before I wandered back to my room. I hoped things would work out for Bev, and I couldn't agree more that she needed to get away from her futile relationship with Rick.

In the room, for some reason I thought about Stu and his problems. If he had come out here like we planned to hike the Rockies, I wondered how everything would have turned out. Perhaps it wouldn't have affected anything, but deep down I believed it was a very good thing that Stu had stayed home. Sure, he had to get better, but unlike Sean and perhaps even Bev, something made me think it wouldn't have been as easy for Stu to handle the past few days.

I started to pack. I was definitely going to leave today.

CHAPTER 25

I took my suitcase out to my car. At some point after I had returned to the lodge last night, it had rained, and puddles now filled any depression they could find. Fortunately, my walk to the car avoided the low spots.

Once back inside I asked how late I could check out. The old man behind the reception counter, an employee I hadn't seen before, told me late checkout would be one o'clock.

"So what do you think of all the excitement around here?" I asked.

"This is my first day back. I think I've managed to miss it all, thank heavens."

"Were you on vacation?"

"No. I retired nearly a year ago, but with all this excitement, as you call it, they needed me back."

"I know a lot of the employees were a little spooked," I said.

"I can't say as I blame them."

"No, me neither," I said. "Well, it's nice that you were able to come in and help them out."

"Can't say the money won't come in handy, too," he said. He almost reminded me of a butler in an English mystery or a dramatic production I might have seen on Masterpiece Theater.

If he had the English accent, he would be a perfect match.

"Have a good day," I said and started back to my room.

"You too, sir."

"Jim," Detective Bruno called when I reached the first step.

I turned and saw him, along with Geri walking out of the dining room.

"Don't tell me you had three breakfasts this morning."

"No, but I could have." He grinned and patted his stomach.

"Morning, Jim," Geri said.

I walked over and met them in the middle of the room.

"And a good morning to you, too."

"I want to thank you again for risking your life for me last night."

"You would have done the same for me," I said.

"I mean it. You and Sean will forever be my heroes," she said.

"Thanks. I'm just glad you're okay."

"I hope so, but I guess it isn't over yet," Geri said. "Detective Bruno says I'll be in danger until Vic is captured."

"I'm only cautioning you. There's little chance that he would chance it, but you have to understand there's still a risk," Detective Bruno explained.

"At this point there's really nothing to be gained for him to come after you," I said. "Last night he believed you were the only one to have figured out he was the killer. By now he has to know that everyone knows about him. Other than vengeance, I can't see any other motive, but Detective Bruno has to make sure you understand that no matter how slight you may still be a target."

"And I do understand that. I wish I could say I know Vic well enough to say what he would or wouldn't do, but apparently, I never knew him very well." She looked at both of us for a second. "He's such a fool. I guess I can no longer put anything past him."

"There you are, Mrs. Schutte."

I looked up and saw Colt Bettes coming down the stairs. She looked at him a little bewildered.

"Geri, do you know Colt Bettes, Sean's cousin?" Before she could answer, I turned to Colt, "Colt, have you officially met Geri?" Although it hadn't appeared to bother her, his calling Geri "Mrs. Schutte" at this point bothered me. It almost seemed like calling her a dirty word. If I was her, I'd be going back to my maiden name as soon as possible.

"Nice to make your acquaintance," he said to Geri. "By any chance, do you have a few minutes to talk to me?"

Rather than answer him she looked at Bruno. "Are we done for now?" she asked.

"Yes, but we'll stay in touch. While you're here, a deputy will always be close by."

"Thanks."

"It will only be a few minutes. I'll be happy to buy you a coffee," Colt persisted.

"Okay," Geri answered and walked off with Colt to the dining room.

I figured Colt wanted to ask her about everything she and Sean did and talked about in the last twelve or so hours. I began to wonder who was more obsessed with Sean's past, Colt or Sean?

Bruno saw Rick enter the lodge and hurried over to speak to him.

I went back to my room to make sure I hadn't forgotten anything. I hadn't. I lay back down on the bed and considered leaving right away. I had planned to stay until early afternoon purely to allow enough time to pass to make sure everyone was okay with my departure. From what I had heard, everyone would be leaving today.

My mind moved through a variety of topics before finally focusing on Vic Schutte. Where would I be if I was him? I'd already be out of the state and heading north. A person could hide in a lot of places. I had been to Alaska on a few occasions and considered it a beautiful state and a place where someone could easily disappear from the law. Yep, that's where I'd be heading.

I must have dozed because the room phone rang and startled me.

"Hello."

"Jim? It's me Sean. I just wanted to call and thank you again for everything."

"Thank me? I thought we worked pretty well as a team. I couldn't have done it without you." I said it as a platitude, but realized right away that it was probably true.

"Yeah, we made a good team, but what I meant was everything, not just last night."

I still didn't think I had done anything.

"Do you think Geri's going to be okay?" I asked to change the subject.

"Yes. She's a fascinating woman. Do you know much about

her?"

"No, not really."

"We talked for hours last night," he said.

"I thought you both would just crash."

"We did sleep," and then because he thought I cared, "we didn't do anything else, you know. We just talked and then fell asleep."

"Yeah, I was exhausted by the time we got back."

"I wasn't," he said.

"You know, your cousin is debriefing Geri down in the dining room right now."

"I wouldn't be surprised. He means well."

"And, are you really doing well?" I asked.

"Yes, like I said before to you, it's almost like I feel a lot younger. I can't explain it, but I know I've turned a corner in my life."

"That's great. When are you leaving?"

"Later today, I think. Geri and I have agreed to meet next month."

"Really?" I asked.

"Yes, in New York City. She's never been there before."

"Sounds serious."

"That's why we want to wait a month."

"That's probably a good idea."

"We hit it off so well. It seems unreal."

I knew he was talking about Geri and himself, and I felt like saying it was all unreal last night.

"I know what you mean," I said instead. "It's best to let everything settle down."

"Do you think Vic will try something stupid?"

"He's already done stupid things, so who really knows, but my guess is his first goal will be to get as far away from here as possible."

"I hope so. I worry about Geri. What if he goes after her?"

"That's why they still have a deputy watching her. The odds are slim, but the Sheriff is not taking anything for granted."

"Yeah, I guess so."

"And you know, now that everyone knows who the killer is, the remaining four guys with her real estate company should help provide some cover for her." I just thought of it while I said it, but it did seem to make sense to me.

"Yeah, that's probably true, too."

"Sean, I've got a few things to take care of before I go, so I just want you to know that I couldn't have done it without you last night."

"You mean we couldn't have done it without each other, right?"

"Exactly."

"Well you take it easy, Jim."

"You too, Sean." We hung up.

Although I didn't really have anything to do when I indicated to Sean that I needed to get off the phone, something serious did pop into my mind after I hung up. I jumped up and headed downstairs to look for Geri.

I didn't have a problem finding her. She sat next to Colt in the middle of the dining room engrossed in conversation. She must not have found Colt as annoying as I did, or else she had become too interested in hearing the background story to let his condescending attitude bother her.

"Hey, Geri," I said as I approached them.

"Yes, Jim," she said looking up at me.

"Jim, could this wait for a second?" Colt asked.

"It will only take a second," I said. "Geri, I just wanted to caution you that if you receive any text from my cell phone, remember I don't have that phone anymore."

It took her a second to grasp what I was saying, but then she nodded. "It might be prudent to ignore any texts from phones I don't recognize."

"That's even better," I said. "Sorry to have interrupted you." I turned and left the room. They didn't ask me to stay, and I wondered why my warning her seemed so important a few minutes ago. She wouldn't have recognized my phone number anyway. I made a mental note to ask Bruno about it the next time I saw him. Vic hadn't taken the purse out of the car with him, so hopefully he left my cell phone on the back seat of the car, too.

The more I thought about it, the more ambivalent I became. A cell phone came in handy if you needed it and if you had a signal. Other than that, it would be nice if nobody could reach out and bother you when you didn't want to be bothered.

CHAPTER 26

At noon, I decided to leave. I wouldn't be that far away if they needed me. I searched the lodge for Bruno, but he had disappeared. I asked a deputy whom I did find to pass along a message to Bruno that I was hitting the road. I also told him that my cell phone might be in the back seat of the car that Vic had used to abduct his wife and me. If they recovered it, I guess I'd like it back.

Bev had already left, and I felt I had said my goodbyes to everyone else. I checked out and was disappointed that the hotel hadn't even discounted the room charges. I made one pit stop in the dining room.

"Susan," I said to her while she cleaned the plates off a table.

"Lunch?" she asked me with a smile.

"No, can I just have a coffee in a to go cup?"

"Sure. You leaving us?"

"Yes. It's time for me to go."

"I understand you were quite the hero last night."

"Not really. Besides, I didn't have much choice."

The way she looked at me before she turned to get my coffee made me wish I was twenty years younger. She returned in a couple of minutes with a cup of coffee and a bag of something.

"It's a sandwich," she said. "It's on the house for helping out my dad."

"Why, thank you. You take care of yourself," I said and left. Helping out her father had been the last thing on my mind the last several days, but I appreciated the sandwich.

I climbed into my car and started to leave when I saw Nesbitt and Stallings standing by the edge of the parking lot. Something else there beside them caught my eye and made me smile. I drove straight for it.

Stallings had his arm up and pointed at something in the distance for Nesbitt to see. It could've been a deer, a hawk, or something else. It didn't matter to me. I was simply happy that whatever it was, it kept their attention away from me.

I hit the mud puddle next to them, and dirty water spayed all over both of them. I never slowed down but caught a satisfying glimpse of them jumping around and trying to shake the water off. Childish revenge, yes, but it made my day.

The first part of my drive out of the Pecos Wilderness Area wound through beautiful forest covered hills and valleys. Elsewhere in the state, the highways can stretch for miles without the slightest bend; here it appeared that the person tasked with laying out a straight road may have been a little tipsy. The highway bent one way or the other about every half mile, if not more often.

Except in the big cities, which are few in New Mexico, traffic is usually light. It made me again wonder how Vic would get out of the state. The Sheriff had said that he had Vic's rental car under surveillance. Most likely, the sheriff wouldn't lift it for another day or so. That left Vic on foot, and one couldn't just hike out of state from the Santa Fe area. New Mexico extended for over a hundred miles in every direction. It might be slightly less if you headed due north, but that would be through the roughest part of the mountains.

Hitchhiking would also be difficult, and more so now than ever since the murders and ongoing manhunt had made the front pages. I guess if I was him, I'd be looking for a car to steal. But then, I wouldn't be him.

Once I hit I-40, the terrain changed and I got back into the New Mexico I had become more accustomed to: miles and miles of nothing, interrupted by a few trees and a house or two. Actually, I liked it. It said to me, like it has always said to me, "What you see is what you get."

I drove on, my mind remembering years ago when I had first returned to New Mexico after the Air Force. This area was close to where I had encountered a news reporter for the small town of Denton. She had rekindled a flame inside me that I thought had been extinguished forever. The two of us were tossed into the midst of a murder investigation. An ugly one, if you could call one more ugly than others.

I had nothing important to do and would have tried to look her up, but I knew she had moved on to bigger jobs and bigger cities back east. Still, as I drove through the small town, I felt the tug.

I turned south on 209, a good road that went south for twenty miles, east for thirty miles, and then straight south again for another thirty before dying in Clovis. Traffic had never been a problem on this road, and I encountered only a few vehicles on this last stretch of my drive home.

Chubbs ran back and forth in the backyard when he heard my car pull into the driveway. You'd think I had been gone a month rather than just a few days. After my obligatory bonding with Chubbs, I walked next door and paid the fourteen year old. She had only recently taken over the responsibility for Chubbs from her older sister. My understanding of the process was that after she received the payment from me, she would ration portions of the money to her younger siblings, supposedly in proportion to the support they provided her.

Her older sister, now sixteen, had moved on to high school and more important endeavors. Sibyl, her mom, had informed me that she had become too fixated on another high school sophomore, a boy, and might not be as reliable as she had once been. So Chubbs and I had a new business partner. Chubbs had no problem with the change in leadership, and I had long known that all the children kept Chubbs busy while I was away.

I called Detective Bruno the day after I returned. I did it mainly as a courtesy and with perhaps a bit of curiosity regarding the search for Vic. He was in a good mood but said that so far no one had seen any sign of Vic. That troubled me only because I knew the longer he could elude the authorities the farther away he could get.

Later that night, I learned exactly how far Vic had traveled. My first hint that something wasn't right came from Chubbs in the form of a low growl. He's normally a barker not a growler, so his growl got my attention right away.

"Shhh," I said softly to him as I sat up in bed.

Another growl.

"Quiet now," I said and stroked his ears. "Let's see what we have out there."

From my bedroom windows I can see most of my back yard. I separated two of the blinds with my fingers and peered along the back of my one story house. Someone definitely crouched at the far end by the door that went into my utility room. The darkness and distance between us prevented me from identifying him, but I immediately had my suspicions.

I reached under my bed and drew out the cutlass that had been collecting dust there since I moved into the house. Years ago, I received it as a gift from a friend in the British MI-5. We had worked together on a particularly nasty espionage case on Gibraltar. Besides the bond we had formed, the final outcome was about the only thing positive that came out of the lengthy investigation. That subsequent Christmas, the cutlass arrived gift wrapped and unexpected at my office.

I knew the cutlass couldn't match a gun, but in close quarters and in my own house, I felt secure with it and a few baseball bats scattered about.

I walked quickly down the hall, stopping before I got to the kitchen to listen. Not a sound came from anywhere until Chubbs, at my feet, growled again.

"Shh, boy, we don't want to scare this one away."

A phone sat on the desk in my library. I dialed 911 but left the receiver on the desk. I knew someone would respond whether I spoke or not.

I crossed the kitchen and paused again at the entry to the utility room. The door to the outside was to my left, and the washer and dryer and bathroom were to my right. I heard a scraping sound coming from the doorway and guessed that he was trying to pop open the door with a chisel or a large screwdriver.

Although I had an alarm system, I rarely used it, but he would have no way to know that. Trying to break into my house was foolhardy. If that was Vic out there, and I was betting money it was, he had certainly become even more irrational. Perhaps he thought that even if I had the alarm on, it would take the authorities at least five minute to respond to my house, and that he could get in, shoot me, and be gone well within five minutes.

But why me? That was another question I would have to think about later, as I heard a crunching sound that indicated that whoever it was out there may have succeeded in getting the door open. Just as the crunching sound reached us, Chubbs let out a nervous yip.

Leaning tight against the wall, I squatted down for a second and calmed Chubbs. His silence amazed me. He usually won't stop barking when anyone even knocks on the door. I heard the door being pushed open and immediately stood up and braced myself against the wall of the kitchen.

For a second nothing seemed to happen. Then it appeared. By it, I'm referring to that large ugly revolver that had already taken a few shots at me. I had hoped it would be the first thing that came into view. A real professional knows not to lead himself around corners with his gun hand, but you see it all the time on TV, so most amateurs have never caught on.

As soon as the revolver came into view, two things happened: Chubbs could no longer control himself and began barking as ferociously as he could, and I slashed the cutlass down and into Vic's wrist. Unlike what you see in the movies, it's not easy to slice an individual's hand off. In my case, I learned later that the cutlass did slice through one bone before the blade got stuck in the second.

The revolver fell to the floor and Vic screamed in pain. He also instinctively jerked away, almost wrenching the cutlass out of my hand. I held on to the cutlass and followed Vic back into the utility room where he collapsed in shock against the far wall. Blood was streaming out of his arm, and I finally had to yank on the cutlass for it to break away from the bone and flesh. Vic screamed again and tried to cover his wounded wrist with his good hand.

I took a step away from him and kicked the revolver into the kitchen and out of sight. Vic didn't appear to notice. He sat there and stared at his wrist. He seemed to be in a daze. Even Chubbs had backed away and sat quietly. I turned on the lights and grabbed a yard towel that had been washed off the top of the dryer. I tossed it to Vic and told him to wrap it tightly around the wound. He looked at me blankly but did as I instructed.

The cops would be here any second, so I hurried into the library, grabbed the phone and returned to Vic. He hadn't moved.

"Hello," I said into the receiver.

The 911 operator answered me. I told her what had happened and asked her to tell the responding police and EMS personnel to come around to the back door. I explained that I didn't want to leave my prisoner alone. I also told her he may have murdered two people already. I turned on the outside light and waited.

"You ass! You nearly cut off my hand!" Vic snarled and moaned, but never made eye contact with me.

"You were going to kill your wife and me. You almost succeeded. I should've cut off your head."

He still didn't look at me but he shut up. I looked down at the cutlass and felt the urge to clean it. I could see how the cutlass was a favorite weapon of a lot of sailors a couple of centuries ago. At close range, it could do a lot of damage.

The flashing lights of the police vehicles bounced off the few trees I had out back and signaled to me the cavalry had arrived. Chubbs, who had been strangely silent for a while, started barking. I hushed Chubbs and told him these were the good guys.

"You're lucky you're still alive, Vic. I imagine you'll be behind bars for a long time, but if by some miracle you are let loose, don't you ever think about hurting another soul. Understand?"

He sat there on my floor holding the towel tightly to his wrist and rocked back and forth. He ignored me, if he heard me at all.

"Hello?" a hesitant voice sounded from outside. "Police here. Mr. West, what's the status inside?"

"Everything's secure. You can come in," I shouted back.

A uniformed patrolman appeared at the door. Another shadow stood behind him off to the side.

"He busted in," I said and pointed to the door frame. "He had a gun. It's on the floor in the kitchen now. His names Vic Schutte. He's wanted for two murders."

The young officer looked at the cutlass in my hand and his eyes widened.

"Is that a machete?"

"No, a genuine replica of an old English cutlass."

"Is that what happened to his hand?"

"Yes," I said. "I imagine you'll want it." I offered it handle first to him, doing my best to avoid the blood on the blade as I did.

He looked at it hesitantly.

"Bert, come on in," he said to his partner. "Get a bag we can put that in." He motioned to the cutlass that I still held. "And another bag for a gun." He looked at me inquisitively.

"A large revolver," I said.

"You okay with everything in here?" the one patrolman asked his partner before disappearing. The officer inside nodded his assent.

"Are you okay, Mr. West?"

"Yes, I'm fine."

"How bad is your hand?" he asked Vic.

Vic didn't answer. He didn't look up.

"It's still attached," I said.

The other patrolman returned, took the cutlass, and then retrieved the revolver. I heard more voices outside and my house soon became the center of a lot of attention. I finally had to put Chubbs back into my bedroom.

They had a real dilemma to solve before they could transport Vic to the hospital. Protocol required some form of wrist restraints, but handcuffs seemed out of the question. They took me to another room to get my statement, so I never did see how they restrained him before moving him. I don't think he had any fight left in him anyway. He had lost a lot of blood, but no one seemed to care.

The police chief eventually showed up at my house. I had met him a few times and we got along.

"I knew that sooner or later you'd bring one of your messes back here to Clovis," he said. I knew he wasn't kidding and I couldn't blame him.

"I didn't bring anything here. It came after me and it makes no sense to me."

"I've been in touch with the state police and the sheriff's office that issued the lookout for this guy. Needless to say, they're all extremely happy that this guy is off the streets."

"Me, too."

"Why do you think he came after you?"

"I don't know. A rather stupid thing for him to do."

"To me, murder is always stupid," the chief said.

"Can't argue that."

He looked around my house without explaining why. I followed him in silence. After he satisfied whatever it was that drove him to want to inspect my house, he walked out front and talked to a couple of his men.

"Jim, have a good one," he said and walked off to his car.

I waved.

CHAPTER 27

The next day, I hired a crew to come out and clean my entire house, with particular attention paid to the utility room. Getting blood off the walls and floors has never been my cup of tea.

I refused to talk to the local press, referring them to the police for any information about the break in at my house or its relationship with the two murders. The editor of the local paper personally called me, but I declined comment which understandably irritated him. I knew he was simply doing his job and I didn't get angry with him. I also realized that my refusal might come back and bite me some day. It never did anyone any good to get on the bad side of the press.

A strange request came to me on the second day after Vic's attempt to kill me which I did accept. About three in the afternoon, I had a call from the local police asking me to come down to their offices. They had made no progress in getting any comment from Vic. Later that evening he would be shipped up to Santa Fe. The local authorities had made a consensus decision to have me talk to Vic before he left town. I would be alone with him in the interview room, but a number of witnesses would be monitoring any conversation we might have.

"Has he asked for an attorney?" I asked when I arrived at the police department.

"He hasn't said anything to us about anything," the chief said.

"Not a single word," echoed another man in civilian clothes who I thought was with the District Attorney's office.

"What do you want me to get him to say?"

"Anything. We'd like for him to open up and say something."

"I'll give it a shot, but I doubt if he'll say anything to me either. We weren't exactly best friends."

"Hey, we've got nothing to lose. At some point he'll lawyer up, and then we'll lose any chance we have at all."

They walked me to an interview room, and I went in. Vic sat there alone, his right forearm and hand in a cast. He stared down at the table in front of him. I wondered if the effects of any medication he might be on were bothering him.

"At least you're not going to lose the hand," I said as I sat down across from him.

He looked up, and I got the sense that my presence had surprised him.

His lips curled. "So you are a cop after all."

"No, I'm not. Why did you break into my house the other night, Vic?"

He looked at me with suspicion for a few seconds before he spoke. "I just wanted to talk to you."

Might not have been the biggest lie I'd ever heard, but it was definitely in the competition.

"About what?"

"I didn't kill anyone up there at the lodge. I just wanted to talk some sense into you. I figured if I could convince you to get off my back, then Geri probably wouldn't testify."

His remarks surprised me, but maybe they shouldn't have. I had no doubt he murdered Cross and Randi. He had already confessed it to both Geri and me, but this approach was for the police who he knew had to be listening in. If you simply changed the word convince to kill, what he said made sense. With me murdered, he might have been able to intimidate Geri into staying silent.

"The police will never find the evidence needed to convict me, but with you and Geri lying about me who knows what a jury might believe."

"Why would we want to lie about you?"

"So you two can have all the money and each other," he said.

"She never wanted me, and you know she doesn't want the money. Besides, I think she has her eyes on someone else already."

His eyes focused sharply on me again. I knew he wanted to ask me who, but he didn't.

"You know you left a trail a mile wide for the police to follow. Now that they have you to focus on, everything you've done in the last year will paint all the picture they need to convict you."

He didn't say anything, and I thought he had retreated back into his shell of silence.

"Do you want to know where you went wrong, Vic?"

"I know where I went wrong, asshole." He leaned close to

me and lowered his voice to a whisper. "Next time you'll never see me coming. You're a dead man. You just don't know it yet."

"Sorry, man, but I don't think you get a next time."

He sat back, clamped his jaw shut, and closed his eyes.

I stared at him for a full minute. I knew he wouldn't have anything else to say. I stood up, and the door behind me opened.

"Not sure if I got anything worthwhile," I said to the chief.

"You got more than we did."

"Did you hear the threat there at the end when he was whispering?"

"Sure. The mikes we have these days are quite good."

"Chief, you've got a call you might want to take," a uniformed police sergeant said from the doorway to the hall.

"Can you stick around until after this call?" he asked me. Before I could answer, he had turned back to the sergeant, "Skip, get Jim a cup of coffee."

I didn't have anything better to do anyway. The coffee tasted like the coffee I had spent years drinking in the military: strong, stale and with just the right amount of grounds floating around in it. I wondered if the guest mugs were cleaned just as inefficiently.

I began to think that the chief may have forgotten me. When he finally appeared, his grin indicated something big had happened.

"They found the .22 rifle they think he used to kill one of the victims up there," he said.

"They did? Where was it?"

"In the rifle case."

"What? I don't follow you? Whose rifle case are we talking about?"

It was his turn to look a little confused. "How many rifle cases were there?"

Not being there, he hadn't seen the eight, maybe more, rifle cases that Cross' hunting group had brought with them to the lodge.

"A whole bunch, but I guess you mean it was found in one of Vic's."

"Yes. The case was a fancy one. It was large enough for a high caliber hunting rifle, but apparently it also had a false bottom to it. The .22 rifle had been tightly secured in a small second compartment. When they searched the rifle cases originally, I guess when they seized all the hunting rifles as you say, they never suspected that there might have been a hidden compartment in any of the cases."

"That makes sense and clears up one of the little mysteries surrounding this whole mess," I said.

CHAPTER 28

When I arrived back home, I had a message on my machine from Detective Bruno. In the message, Bruno said that my cell phone had been mailed to me and that they had discovered the murder weapon. He also said to call if I wanted to chat.

I thought about it for a while but decided against calling him. I wanted to put some distance between me and the entire investigation. I didn't think I'd be allowed to stay away from it for very long, so it therefore surprised me about a month later when I heard Vic and his lawyer were working to cut a deal with the prosecution. It was early in the process, but the prosecutor wanted a minimum of twenty years without a chance for parole, and it sounded like Vic was willing to accept that. The discovery of the weapon used to kill Cross had dampened Vic's confidence that he could beat the rap.

I also heard later from Sean that Geri and he had a nice holiday in New York. For some reason, I felt they would make a good match for each other.

I never heard from Bev, but I considered that to be a good thing. I feared any note that I received from Bev would be to tell me it hadn't worked out. Bev needed to settle down with someone who was right for her and to be happy. Her rancher friend had sounded like a good choice. And, while it was nice to hear that Sean and Geri were doing well, no news from Bev was just fine. Like the old saying goes, no news is good news.

Chubbs dropped the ball he had retrieved after I had thrown it in our backyard and ran to the gate of the fence. He watched in interest as a small white poodle and its master walked down the sidewalk.

"What do you think, buddy? Is she the one for you?" I asked.

He barked once but came back to me and our game of fetch. I took the ball and scratched him behind his ears.

"That's alright. There's always you and me, buddy, always you and me."

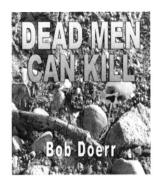

Title: *Dead Men Can Kill*™
Author: Bob Doerr
Price: $27.95
Publisher: TotalRecall Publications, Inc.
Format: HARDCOVER, 6.14" x 9.21"
Number of pages: 320
13-digit ISBN: 978-1-59095-758-5
Publication: December 8, 2009

When Jim West, a former Air Force Special Agent with the Office of Special Investigations, moves back to New Mexico, his goal is simple: start an easy going second career as a professional lecturer on investigative techniques to colleges and civic organizations. He never envisioned that his practical demonstration of forensic hypnosis on stage with a state university student would stir up memories of an 18-year old murder mystery. When the student is murdered three days later, West finds himself ensnared in a web of intrigue that pits him and the small town's authorities against a ruthless, psychotic killer.

An aggressive reporter for the town newspaper seeks out West for help with the story, but after one of her co-workers is murdered, she quickly aligns her efforts with West and the Sheriff. As West works closely with her, he begins to wonder if this could be the first real relationship for him since his devastating divorce a few years earlier.

The killer, though, has other plans for the reporter and the story takes fascinating twists and turns, leading to an inevitable, riveting confrontation.

Look out for a new hero on the mystery/thriller landscape! Jim West, retired military investigator, is resourceful, intuitive, pragmatic and always competent. All of West's abilities are tested when he matches wits with psychopathic serial killer William White, a man whose appreciation for murder is surpassed only by his delight in domination. Bob Doerr has crafted a must-read addition to the genre in Dead Men Can Kill, which evolves from absorbing story to absolute page-turner as West closes in on a killer who is supposedly dead. Highly recommended!

--Dallin Malmgren, author of...

The Whole Nine Yards   The Ninth Issue   Is This for a Grade?

A Jim West™ Mystery/Thriller

Title: *Cold Winter's Kill™*
Author: Bob Doerr
Price: $27.95
Publisher: TotalRecall Publications, Inc.
Format: HARDCOVER, 6.14" x 9.21"
Number of pages: 288
13-digit ISBN: 978-1-59095-762-8
Publication: Dec 8, 2009

Cold Winter's Kill is a fast paced thriller that takes place in the scenic mountains of Lincoln County, New Mexico and throws Jim West into a race against time to stop a psychopath who abducts and kills a young blonde every Christmas...

It was one of those phone calls former Air Force Special Agent Jim West never wanted to receive--an old friend calling to ask if he could drive down to Ruidoso, New Mexico to help locate his daughter who has disappeared while on a ski trip with friends. Jim found himself heading to Ruidoso even though he believed, much like the local authorities, that if she had gone missing in the mountains in December, her survival chances were slim. He didn't want to be there when they found her, but still he drove on.

Once in Ruidoso, Jim discovers a sinister coincidence that changes everything. It appears that someone is abducting and killing one young blond every year around Christmas. The race is on--can Jim locate his friend's daughter in time? But why is this happening and who's doing it?

Jim can't wait for the local authorities to raise the priority of their search, or for the pending blizzard to pass. In his haste he puts himself in the killer's sights. Will he, too, suffer from a cold winter's kill?

"GREAT SUSPENSE! In *Cold Winter's Kill* Bob Doerr grabs your attention from the beginning and holds it until the last sentence. Hard to put down!"
   --Shelba Nicholson
      former Women's Editor, *Texarkana Gazette*

Author Bob Doerr Uses his special knowledge to provide authentic details in his novels about how law enforcement agencies do their work.

A Jim West™ Mystery/Thriller

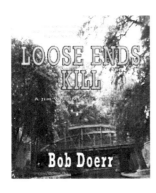

Title: *Loose Ends Kill*™
Author: Bob Doerr
Price: $27.95
Publisher: TotalRecall Publications, Inc.
Format: HARDCOVER, 6.14" x 9.21"
Number of pages: 288
13-digit ISBN: 978-1-59095-717-2
Publication: Oct 27, 2010

LOOSE ENDS KILL is a fast paced mystery/thriller that takes place in the historic city of San Antonio, Texas, and throws Jim West into the middle of a police investigation of the murder of an old friend's wife. The police already believe they have the killer in custody – West's friend.

West is drawn into this mystery by a call from the old friend who requests his assistance. West agrees to help his friend and digs deep to try to find another suspect. In the process he soon discovers that he is being followed and targeted for harassment, but by whom?

West quickly discovers that he didn't know his old friend's wife as well as he thought. To his surprise, he learns that she has had a number of affairs dating back for more than a decade. In fact, while investigating the murder, he realizes that his friend and he may be the only two people unaware of her philandering behavior.

Theorizing that one of her lovers could have had just as much motive as her husband, West starts turning over the rocks identifying one lover after another. In doing so, West unintentionally ignites an outbreak of more death and mayhem. The police and his friend's lawyers want West to go back home. The police even threaten to arrest him.

Soon, West believes the real killer wants him gone or dead. Deciding the only way to resolve the case before the outside pressures force him to leave, he sets a trap for the killer using himself as bait. However, he soon learns he may have only outsmarted himself.

A Jim West™ Mystery/Thriller

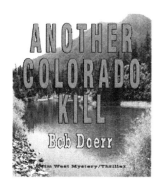

Title: *Another Colorado Kill*™
Author: Bob Doerr
Price: $27.95
Publisher: TotalRecall Publications, Inc.
Format: HARDCOVER, 6.14" x 9.21"
Number of pages in the finished book: 288
13-digit ISBN: 978-1-59095-784-4
Publication Date: September 06, 2011

It was supposed to be a short, fun golf outing, but when Jim West and his friend Edward "Perry" Mason stumble across a dead body in a restroom at a rest stop along I-25, things turn bad and then only get worse.

With the golf outing shot, West intends to stay in Colorado Springs only for a day or two. However, when two more murder victims turn up – one with West's name handwritten in her notebook - the heat on West skyrockets. The police instruct him to stick around, and soon he discovers that while the police may want to pin the crimes on him, the killer wants him out of the picture. Way out – like dead.

West's only ally is Lieutenant Michelle Prado, a tall red head with large green eyes that captivate West. Assigned to keep an eye on West, Lieutenant Prado decides the best way to do so is to keep him close. West and Prado do their own digging into the investigation. In the process, Jim wonders how close their relationship will evolve.

It seems to West that as the police focus less on him, the killer intensifies his focus on him. Barely surviving an initial confrontation, West realizes he must take the initiative. If he doesn't, or perhaps even if he does - he may end up as just another Colorado kill.

A Jim West™ Mystery/Thriller
www.bobdoerr.com

CPSIA information can be obtained at www.ICGtesting.com
Printed in the USA
LVOW08*1222201214

419008LV00001B/8/P

9 781590 954225